GEORGES SIMENON

Pietr the Latvian

Translated by DAVID BELLOS

PENGUIN BOOKS

PENGUIN CLASSICS

Published by the Penguin Group
Penguin Books Ltd, 80 Strand, London WC2R ORL, England
Penguin Group (USA) Inc., 375 Hudson Street, New York, New York 10014, USA
Penguin Group (Canada), 90 Eglinton Avenue East, Suite 700, Toronto, Ontario, Canada M4P 2Y3
(a division of Pearson Penguin Canada Inc.)
Penguin Ireland, 25 St Stephen's Green, Dublin 2, Ireland (a division of Penguin Books Ltd)
Penguin Group (Australia), 707 Collins Street, Melbourne, Victoria 3008, Australia
(a division of Pearson Australia Group Pty Ltd)
Penguin Books India Pvt Ltd, 11 Community Centre, Panchsheel Park, New Delhi – 110 017, India
Penguin Group (NZ), 67 Apollo Drive, Rosedale, Auckland 0632, New Zealand
(a division of Pearson New Zealand Ltd)
Penguin Books (South Africa) (Pty) Ltd, Block D, Rosebank Office Park, 181 Jan Smuts Avenue,
Parktown North, Gauteng 2193, South Africa

Penguin Books Ltd, Registered Offices: 80 Strand, London WC2R ORL, England

www.penguin.com

First published in serial, as *Pietr-le-Letton*, in *Ric et Rac* 1930
This translation first published 2013
004

Copyright 1930 by Georges Simenon Limited
Translation © David Bellos, 2013
GEORGES SIMENON ® Simenon.tm
MAIGRET ® Georges Simenon Limited
All rights reserved

The moral rights of the author and translator have been asserted

Set in 11 / 13pt Dante by Palimpsest Book Production Limited, Falkirk, Stirlingshire
Printed in Great Britain by Clays Ltd, St Ives plc

ISBN: 978-0-141-39273-8

www.greenpenguin.co.uk

MIX
Paper from
responsible sources
FSC
www.fsc.org   FSC™ C018179

Penguin Books is committed to a sustainable
future for our business, our readers and our planet.
This book is made from Forest Stewardship
Council™ certified paper.

1. *Apparent age 32, height 169 . . .*

ICPC to PJ Paris Xvzust Krakow vimontra m ghks triv psot uv
Pietr-le-Letton Bremen vs tyz btolem.

Detective Chief Inspector Maigret of the Flying Squad
raised his eyes. It seemed to him that the cast-iron stove
in the middle of his office with its chimney tube rising to
the ceiling wasn't roaring properly. He pushed the telegram away, rose ponderously to his feet, adjusted the flue
and thrust three shovels of coal into the firebox.

Then he stood with his back to the stove, filled his pipe
and adjusted his stud collar, which was irritating his neck
even though it wasn't set very high.

He glanced at his watch. Four p.m. His jacket was hanging on a hook on the back of the door.

Slowly he returned to his desk, mouthing a translation
as he went:

> International Criminal Police Commission to Police Judi-
> ciaire in Paris: Krakow police report sighting Pietr the
> Latvian en route to Bremen.

The International Criminal Police Commission, or ICPC,
is based in Vienna. Broadly speaking, it oversees the struggle against organized crime in Europe, with a particular
responsibility for liaison between the various national
police forces on the Continent.

Maigret pulled up another telegram that was similarly written in IPC, the secret international police code used for communication between all the world's police forces. He translated at sight:

Polizei-Präsidium Bremen to PJ Paris: Pietr the Latvian reported en route Amsterdam and Brussels.

Another telegram from the Nederlandsche Centrale in Zake Internationale Misdadigers, the Dutch police HQ, reported:

At 11 a.m. Pietr the Latvian boarded Étoile du Nord, compartment G. 263, car 5, destination Paris.

The final message in IPC had been sent from Brussels and said:

Confirm Pietr the Latvian on board Étoile du Nord via Brussels 2 a.m. in compartment reported by Amsterdam.

Behind Maigret's desk there was a huge map pinned to the wall. The inspector was a broad and heavy man. He stood staring at the map with his hands in his pockets and his pipe sticking out the side of his mouth.

His eyes travelled from the dot representing Krakow to the other dot showing the port of Bremen and from there to Amsterdam and Paris.

He checked the time once again. Four-twenty. The Étoile du Nord should now be hurtling along at sixty miles an hour between Saint-Quentin and Compiègne.

It wouldn't stop at the border. It wouldn't be slowing down.

In car 5, compartment G. 263, Pietr the Latvian was presumably spending his time reading or looking at the scenery.

Maigret went over to a door that opened onto a closet,

washed his hands in an enamel basin, ran a comb through thick dark-brown hair flecked with only a few silver strands around the temple, and did his best to straighten out his tie – he'd never learned how to do a proper knot.

It was November and it was getting dark. Through the window he could see a branch of the Seine, Place Saint-Michel, and a floating wash-house, all in a blue shroud speckled by gas lamps lighting up one after the other.

He opened a drawer and glanced at a dispatch from the International Identification Bureau in Copenhagen.

Paris PJ Pietr-le-Letton 32 169 01512 0224 0255 02732 03116 03233 03243 03325 03415 03522 04115 04144 04147 05221 . . .

This time he made an effort to speak the translation aloud and even went over it several times, like a schoolchild reciting a lesson:

Description Pietr the Latvian: apparent age 32 years, height 169 cm, sinus top straight line, bottom flat, extension large max, special feature septum not visible, ear unmarked rim, lobe large, max cross and dimension small max, protuberant antitragus, vex edge lower fold, edge shape straight line edge feature separate lines, orthognathous upper, long face, biconcave, eyebrows thin fair light, lower lip jutting max thick lower droop, light.

This 'word-picture' of Pietr was as clear as a photograph to Inspector Maigret. The principal features were the first to emerge: the man was short, slim, young and fair-haired, with sparse blond eyebrows, greenish eyes and a long neck.

Maigret now also knew the shape of his ear in the minutest detail. This would enable him to make a positive identification in a milling crowd even if the suspect was in disguise.

He took his jacket off the hook and slipped his arms into it, then put on a heavy black overcoat and a bowler hat.

One last glance at the stove, which seemed on the verge of exploding.

At the end of the corridor, on the stair landing that was used as a waiting room, he reminded Jean:

'You won't forget to keep my stove going, will you?'

The wind swirling up the stairs took him by surprise, and he had to shelter from the draught in a corner to get his pipe to light.

Wind and rain blew in squalls over the platforms of Gare du Nord despite the monumental glass canopy overhead. Several panes had blown out and lay in shards on the railway tracks. The lighting wasn't working properly. People huddled up inside their clothes.

Outside one of the ticket windows an alarming travel notice had been posted:

Channel forecast: gale-force winds.

One woman, whose son was to catch the Folkestone boat train, looked upset; her eyes were red. She kept on telling the boy what he should do, right up to the last minute. In his embarrassment he had no choice but to promise not to go out on deck.

Maigret stood near platform 11 where people were awaiting the arrival of the Étoile du Nord. All the leading hotels, as well as Thomas Cook, had their agents standing by.

He stood still. Other people were agitated. A young

woman clad in mink yet wearing only sheer silk stockings walked up and down, stamping her heels.

He just stood there: a hulk of a man, with shoulders so broad as to cast a wide shadow. When people bumped into him he stayed as firm as a brick wall.

The yellow speck of the train's headlamp appeared in the distance. Then came the usual hubbub, with porters shouting and passengers tramping and jostling their way towards the station exit.

A couple of hundred passengers paraded past Maigret before he picked out in the crowd a short man wearing a broad-checked green travelling cape of a distinctly Nordic cut and colour.

The man wasn't in a hurry. He had three porters behind him. Bowing and scraping, an agent from one of the grand hotels on the Champs-Élysées cleared the way in front of him.

Apparent age 32, height 169 . . . sinus top . . .

Maigret kept calm. He looked hard at the man's ear. That was all he needed.

The man in green passed close by. One of his porters bumped Maigret with one of the suitcases.

At exactly the same moment a railway employee began to run, shouting out something to his colleague standing at the station end of the platform, next to the barrier.

The chain was drawn closed. Protests erupted.

The man in the travelling cape was already out of the station.

Maigret puffed away at his pipe in quick short bursts. He went up to the official who had closed the barrier.

'Police! What's happened?'

'A crime . . . They've just found . . .'

'Carriage 5? . . .'

'I think so . . .'

The station went about its regular business; only platform II looked abnormal. There were fifty passengers still waiting to get out, but their path was blocked. They were getting excited.

'Let them go . . .' Maigret said.

'But . . .'

'Let them go . . .'

He watched the last cluster move away. The station loudspeaker announced the departure of a local train. Somebody was running somewhere. Beside one of the carriages of the Étoile du Nord there was a small group waiting for something. Three of them, in railway company livery.

The stationmaster got to them first. He was a large man and had a worried look on his face. Then a hospital stretcher was wheeled through the main hall, past clumps of people who looked at it uneasily, especially those about to depart.

Maigret walked up the side of the train with his usual heavy tread, smoking as he went. Carriage I, carriage 2 . . . He came to carriage 5.

That's where the group was standing at the door. The stretcher came to a halt. The stationmaster tried to listen to the three men, who were all speaking at the same time.

'Police! Where is he?'

Maigret's presence provided obvious relief. He propelled his placid mass towards the centre of the frantic group. The other men instantly became his satellites.

'In the toilet . . .'

Maigret hauled himself up onto the train and saw that

6

the toilet door on his right was open. On the floor, in a heap, was a body, bent double in a strangely contorted posture.

The conductor was giving orders from the platform.

'Shunt the carriage to the yard . . . Hang on! . . . Track 62 . . . Let the railway police know . . .'

At first he could only see the back of the man's neck. But when he tipped his cap off its oblique angle, he could see the man's left ear. Maigret mumbled to himself: *lobe large, max cross and dimension small max, protuberant antitragus . . .*

There were a few drops of blood on the linoleum. Maigret looked around. The railway staff were standing on the platform or on the running board. The stationmaster was still talking.

So Maigret clenched his pipe between his teeth even harder and turned the man's head over.

If he hadn't seen the traveller in the green cloak leave the station, if he hadn't seen him taken to a car by an interpreter from the Majestic, he could have had doubts.

It was the same physiognomy. The same fair toothbrush moustache under a sharply defined nose. The same sparse blond eyebrows. The same grey-green eyes.

In other words: Pietr the Latvian!

Maigret could hardly turn around in the tiny washroom, where the tap was still running and a jet of steam was seeping from some poorly sealed joint.

He was standing right next to the corpse. He pulled the man's upper body upright and saw on his chest, on his jacket and shirt, the burn-marks made by gunshot from point-blank range.

It was a big blackish stain tinged with the dark red of coagulating blood.

*

One detail struck the inspector. He happened to notice one of the man's feet. It was twisted on its side, as was the whole body, which must have been squashed into a corner so as to allow the door to close.

The shoe was black and happened to be of a very cheap and common kind. Apparently it had been re-soled. The heel was worn on one side, and a coin-shaped gap had opened up in the middle of the sole.

The local chief of the railway police had now reached the carriage and was calling up from the platform. He was a self-confident man wearing a uniform with epaulettes.

'So what is it, then? Murder? Suicide? Don't touch anything until the law gets here, OK? Be careful! I'm the one who's in charge. OK?'

Maigret had a tough time disentangling his own feet from the dead man's legs to extricate himself from the toilet. With swift, professional movements he patted the man's pockets. Clean as a whistle. Nothing in them at all.

He got out of the carriage, His pipe had gone out, his hat was askew and he had a bloodstain on his cuff.

'Well, if it isn't Maigret! . . . What do you make of it, then?'

'Not much. Go have a look yourself . . .'

'It's suicide, right?'

'If you say so . . . Did you call the prosecutor's office?'

'As soon as I heard . . .'

The loudspeaker crackled with some message or other. A few people had noticed there was something unusual going on and stood in the distance, watching the empty train and the group of people standing next to the running board of carriage 5.

Maigret strode off without saying a word. He left the station and hailed a cab.

'Hôtel Majestic! . . .'

The storm had got even worse. Gusts swept down the streets and made pedestrians totter about like drunks. A roof tile smashed onto the pavement. Buses, and more buses.

The Champs-Élysées was almost entirely deserted. Drops of rain had begun to fall. The porter at the Majestic dashed out to the taxi with a huge red umbrella.

'Police! . . . Has someone from the Étoile du Nord just checked in?'

That prompted the porter to fold his umbrella.

'Yes, sir, that true.'

'Green cape . . . Fair moustache . . .'

'That right. Sir go reception.'

People were scrambling to shelter from the rain. Maigret got inside the hotel just in time to avoid drops as big as walnuts and cold as ice.

Despite this, the receptionists and interpreters behind the polished wood counter were as elegant and efficient as ever.

'Police . . . A guest in a green cape . . . Small fair mousta—'

'Room 17, sir. His bags are on their way up right now . . .'

2. Mixing with Millionaires

Inevitably Maigret was a hostile presence in the Majestic. He constituted a kind of foreign body that the hotel's atmosphere could not assimilate.

Not that he looked like a cartoon policeman. He didn't have a moustache and he didn't wear heavy boots. His clothes were well cut and made of fairly light worsted. He shaved every day and looked after his hands.

But his frame was proletarian. He was a big, bony man. Iron muscles shaped his jacket sleeves and quickly wore through new trousers.

He had a way of imposing himself just by standing there. His assertive presence had often irked many of his own colleagues.

It was something more than self-confidence but less than pride. He would turn up and stand like a rock with his feet wide apart. On that rock all would shatter, whether Maigret moved forward or stayed exactly where he was.

His pipe was nailed to his jawbone. He wasn't going to remove it just because he was in the lobby of the Majestic.

Could it be that Maigret simply preferred to be common and self-assertive?

You just couldn't miss the man wearing a big black velvet-collared overcoat in that brightly lit lobby, where excitable society ladies scattered trails of perfume, tinkling laughter and loud whispers amidst the unctuous compliments of impeccable flunkeys.

He paid no attention. He wasn't part of the flow. He was impervious to the sound of jazz floating up from the dance-floor in the basement.

The inspector started to go up one of the stairs. A liftboy called out and asked if he wanted to take the lift, but Maigret didn't even turn round.

At the first landing someone asked him:

'Are you looking for . . . ?'

It was as is if the sound waves hadn't reached him. He glanced at the corridors with their red carpets stretching out so far that they almost made you sick. He went on up.

On the second floor he read the numbers on the bronze plaques. The door of no. 17 was open. Valets with striped waistcoats were bringing in the luggage.

The traveller had taken off his cloak and looked very slender and elegant in his pinstripe suit. He was smoking a papirosa and giving instructions at the same time.

No. 17 wasn't a room, but a whole suite: lounge, study, bedroom and bathroom. The doors opened onto two intersecting corridors, and at the corner, like a bench placed by a crossroads, there was a huge, curved sofa.

That's where Maigret sat himself down, right opposite the open door. He stretched out his legs and unbuttoned his overcoat.

Pietr saw him and, showing neither surprise nor disquiet, he carried on giving instructions. When the valets had finished placing his trunks and cases on stands, he came to the door, held it open for an instant to inspect the detective, then closed it himself.

Maigret sat there for as long as it took to smoke three

pipes, and to dismiss two room-service waiters and one chambermaid who came up to inquire what he was waiting for.

On the stroke of eight Pietr the Latvian came out of his room, looking even slimmer and smarter than before, in a classically tailored dinner jacket that must have come from Savile Row.

He was hatless. His short, ash-blond hair was already thinning. His hairline was set far back and his forehead not especially high; you could glimpse a streak of pink scalp along the parting.

He had long, pale hands. On the fourth finger of his left hand he wore a chunky platinum signet ring set with a yellow diamond.

He was smoking again – another papirosa. He walked right up to Maigret, stopped for a moment, looked at him as if he felt like saying something, then walked on towards the lift as if lost in thought.

Ten minutes later he took his seat in the dining room at the table of Mr and Mrs Mortimer-Levingston. The latter was the centre of attention: she had pearls worth a cool million on her neck.

The previous day her husband had come to the rescue of one of France's biggest automobile manufacturers, with the result that he was now its majority shareholder.

The three of them were chatting merrily. Pietr talked a lot, but discreetly, with his head leaning forwards. He was completely at ease, natural and casual, despite being able to see the detective's dark outline through the glazed partition.

Inspector Maigret asked reception to show him the guest list. He wasn't surprised to see that Pietr had signed in under the name of Oswald Oppenheim, ship-owner, from Bremen.

It was a foregone conclusion that he had a genuine passport and full identity papers in that name, just as he no doubt did in several others.

It was equally obvious that he'd met the Mortimer-Levingstons previously, whether in Berlin, Warsaw, London or New York.

Was the sole purpose of his presence in Paris to rendez-vous with them and to get away with another one of the colossal scams that were his trademark?

Maigret had the Latvian's file card in his jacket pocket. It said:

Extremely clever and dangerous. Nationality uncertain, from Baltic area. Reckoned to be either Latvian or Estonian. Fluent in Russian, French, English and German. High level of education. Thought to be capo of major international ring mainly involved in fraud. The ring has been spotted successively in Paris, Amsterdam (Van Heuvel case), Berne (United Shipowners affair), Warsaw (Lipmann case) and in various other European cities where identification of its methods and procedures was less clear.

Pietr the Latvian's associates seem to be mainly British and American. One who has been seen most often with him and who was identified when he presented a forged cheque for cash at the Federal Bank in Berne was killed during arrest. His alias was Major Howard of the American Legion, but it has been established that he was actually a former New York bootlegger known in the USA as Fat Fred.

Pietr the Latvian has been arrested twice. First, in

Wiesbaden, for swindling a Munich trader out of half a million marks; second, in Madrid, for a similar offence involving a leading figure at the Spanish royal court.

On both occasions he used the same ploy. He met his victims and presumably told them that the stolen sums were safely hidden and that having him arrested would not reveal where they were. Both times the complaint was withdrawn, and the plaintiffs were probably paid off.

Since then has never been caught red-handed.

Is probably in cahoots with the Maronnetti gang (counterfeit money and forged documents) and the Cologne gang (the 'wall-busters').

There was another rumour doing the rounds of European police departments: Pietr, as the ring-leader and money-launderer of one or more gangs, was said to be sitting on several million that had been split up under different names in different banks and even invested in legitimate industries.

The man smiled subtly at the story Mrs Mortimer-Levingston was telling, while with his ivory hand he plucked luscious grapes from the bunch on his plate.

'Excuse me, sir. Could I please have a word with you?'

Maigret was speaking to Mortimer-Levingston in the lobby of the Majestic after Pietr and Mortimer's wife had both gone back up to their rooms.

Mortimer didn't have the athletic look of a Yank. He was more of the Mediterranean type.

He was tall and thin. His very small head was topped with black hair parted down the middle.

He looked permanently tired. His eyelids were weary and blue. In any case he led an exhausting life, somehow managing to turn up in Deauville, Miami, Venice, Paris,

Cannes and Berlin before getting back to his yacht and then dashing off to do a deal in some European capital or to referee a major boxing match in New York or California.

He looked Maigret up and down in lordly fashion.

'And you are . . . ?'

'Detective Chief Inspector Maigret of the Flying Squad . . .'

Mortimer barely frowned and stood there leaning forwards as if he had decided to grant just one second of his time.

'Are you aware you have just dined with Pietr the Latvian?'

'Is that all you have to say?'

Maigret didn't budge an inch. It was pretty much what he'd expected.

He put his pipe back in his mouth – he'd allowed himself to remove it in order to speak to the millionaire – and muttered:

'That's all.'

He looked pleased with himself. Levingston moved off icily and got into the lift.

It was just after 9.30. The symphony orchestra that had been playing during dinner yielded the stage to a jazz band. People were coming in from outside.

Maigret hadn't eaten. He was standing calmly and patiently in the middle of the lobby. The manager repeatedly gave him worried and disapproving looks from a distance. Even the lowliest members of staff scowled as they passed by, when they didn't manage to jostle him.

The Majestic could not stomach him. Maigret persisted in being a big black unmoving stain amidst the gilding, the chandeliers, the comings and goings of silk evening gowns, fur coats and perfumed, sparkling silhouettes.

Mrs Levingston was the first to come back down in the lift. She had changed, and now wore a lamé cape lined with ermine that left her shoulders bare.

She seemed astonished not to find anyone waiting for her and began to walk up and down, drumming the floor with her gold-lacquered high heels.

She suddenly stopped at the polished wooden counter where the receptionists and interpreters stood and said a few words. One of the staff pushed a red button and picked up a handset.

He looked surprised and called a bellboy, who rushed to the lift.

Mrs Mortimer-Levingston was visibly anxious. Through the glass door you could see the sleek shape of an American-made limousine standing at the kerb.

The bellboy reappeared, spoke to the member of staff, who in his turn said something to Mrs Mortimer. She protested. She must have been saying:

'But that's impossible!'

Maigret then went up the staircase, stopped outside suite 17, knocked on the door. As he'd expected after the circus he'd just watched, there was no answer.

He opened the door and found the lounge deserted. Pietr's dinner jacket was lying casually on the bed in the bedroom. One trunk was open. A pair of patent-leather shoes had been left at opposite ends of the carpet.

The manager came in and grunted:

'You're already here, are you?'

'So? . . . Vanished, has he? Levingston as well! Is that right?'

'Now there's no need to go overboard. Neither of them is in his room, but we'll probably find them somewhere else in the hotel.'

'How many exits are there?'

'Three. The main entrance on the Champs-Élysées . . . Then there's the entrance in the covered mall, and the service entrance on Rue de Ponthieu . . .'

'Is there a security guard? Call him . . .'

The telephone worked. The manager was in a temper. He took it out on an operator who couldn't understand him. He kept his gaze fixed on Maigret, and it was not kind.

'What does all this mean?' he asked as he waited for the guard to come up from the glass-walled box where he was on duty beside the service entrance.

'Nothing, or almost, as you said . . .'

'I hope there's not been a . . . a . . .'

The word *crime*, dreaded like the plague by hoteliers the world over from the humblest lodging-house landlord to the manager of a luxury resort, just would not pass his lips.

'We'll find out.'

Mrs Mortimer-Levingston appeared.

'Well? . . .' she inquired.

The manager bowed and muttered something. A figure appeared at the far end of the corridor – an old man with a straggly beard and ill-cut clothes at odds with the luxurious appearance of the hotel. He was obviously meant to stay in the back, otherwise he too would have been given a fine uniform and been sent to the barber every day.

'Did you see anyone go out?'

'When?'

'In the last few minutes . . .'

'A guy from the kitchen, I think . . . I wasn't paying attention . . . A guy with a cap . . .'

'Was he short? Fair?' Maigret interrupted.

17

'Yes . . . I think so . . . I wasn't watching . . . He was quick . . .'

'Nobody else?'

'I dunno . . . I went round the corner to buy the paper . . .'

Mrs Mortimer-Levingston began to lose her temper.

'Well now! Is that how you conduct a manhunt?' she said to Maigret. 'I've just been told you're a policeman . . . My husband might have been killed . . . What are you waiting for?'

The look that then fell upon her was Maigret through and through! Completely calm! Completely unruffled! It was as if he'd just noticed the buzzing of a bee. As if what he had before him was something quite ordinary.

She was not accustomed to being looked at in that way. She bit her lip, blushed crimson beneath her make-up and stamped her heel with impatience.

He was still staring at her.

Because he was pushing her to the limit, or perhaps because she didn't know what else to do, Mrs Mortimer-Levingston threw a fit.

3. The Strand of Hair

It was nearly midnight when Maigret got back to his office on Quai des Orfèvres. The storm was at its peak. The trees on the riverbank were rattling back and forth and the wash-house barge was tossing about in the waves.

The building was almost empty. At least Jean was still at his post in the lobby at the entrance to a corridor of empty offices.

Voices could be heard coming from the duty room. Then, further down, there was light streaking out from beneath a door – a detective or an inspector working on some case. One of the official cars in the courtyard below was running its engine.

'Is Torrence back?' Maigret asked.

'He's just come in.'

'My stove?'

'It was so hot in your office I had to open the window. There was condensation running down your wall!'

'Get me some beers and sandwiches. None of that soft white bread, mind you.'

He pushed a door and called out:

'Torrence!'

Detective Torrence followed his chief to his office. Before he'd left Gare du Nord Maigret had called Torrence on the telephone and told him to keep going on the case on his own.

Inspector Maigret was forty-five and his junior was barely thirty years old. Even so, there was something solid and bulky about Torrence that made him an almost full-scale model of his boss.

They'd conducted many cases together without ever saying an unnecessary word.

Maigret took off his overcoat and his jacket and loosened his tie. He stood for a while with his back to the stove to let the heat seep in. Then he asked:

'So?'

'The Prosecution Service had an emergency meeting. Forensics took photographs but couldn't find any fingerprints – except the dead man's, of course. They don't match any we have on record.'

'If I remember correctly, don't they have a file on our friend from the Baltic?'

'Just the "word-picture". No fingerprints, no anthropometric data.'

'So we can't be sure that the dead man is someone other than Pietr.'

'But there's no guarantee that it *is* him, either!'

Maigret had taken out his pipe and a pouch that had only a sprinkling of brown dust left in it. Mechanically Torrence handed him an opened packet of shag.

There was a pause. Tobacco crackled in Maigret's pipe. Then came a sound of footsteps and tinkling glassware on the other side of the door, which Torrence opened.

The waiter from Brasserie Dauphine brought in six glasses of beer and four thick-stuffed sandwiches on a tray, which he laid on the table.

'Are you sure that'll be enough?' he asked, seeing that Maigret had company.

'That's fine.'

Maigret started drinking and munching without putting his pipe out, though he did push a glass over to his assistant's side of the desk.

'Well?'

'I questioned all the staff who were on the train. There's definite proof that someone was on board without a ticket. Could be the victim, could be the culprit! We're assuming he got on at Brussels, on the track side. It's easier to hide in a Pullman car than in any other because each carriage has a lot of luggage space. Pietr had tea in the restaurant car between Brussels and the French border and spent his time flicking through a pile of French and English newspapers, including the financial dailies. He went to the toilet between Maubeuge and Saint-Quentin. The head waiter remembers that because as he went past him Pietr said, "Take a whisky to my seat".'

'And he went back to his seat later on?'

'Fifteen minutes later, he was back at his regular place with a whisky in front of him. But the head waiter didn't see Pietr again, since he didn't go back by way of the restaurant car.'

'Did anybody try to use the toilet after him?'

'Sure! A lady traveller tried to get in, but the lock was jammed. It wasn't until the train got to Paris that a staff member managed to force it open. The mechanism had been clogged with iron filings.'

'Up to that point, had anybody set eyes on the second Pietr?'

'Absolutely not. He would have been very noticeable. He was wearing shoddy clothes and would have stood out a mile on a de luxe express.'

'What about the bullet?'

'Shot at point-blank range. Automatic revolver, 6 mm. The shot caused such burning of the skin that according to the doctor the victim would have died from the heat shock alone.'

'Any sign of a struggle?'

'None at all. The pockets were empty.'

'I know that . . .'

'Sorry! However, I did find this in a small button-down pocket on the inside of his waistcoat.'

Torrence then extracted from his wallet a folded piece of transparent paper inside which you could see a strand of brown hair.

'Hand it over . . .'

Maigret hadn't stopped eating and drinking all the while.

'A woman's hair? Or a child's?'

'Forensics says it's a woman's hair. I left him a few strands that he's promised to examine closely.'

'And the autopsy?'

'All done by 10 a.m. Probable age: thirty-two. Height 1 m 68 cm. No hereditary abnormalities. One of his kidneys was in poor shape, which could mean he was a boozer. Stomach contained tea and other digested matter that couldn't be identified straight away. They'll work on the analysis tomorrow. Now the examination is over the body is being kept on ice at the morgue.'

Maigret wiped his mouth, stationed himself in his favourite position in front of the stove and held out his hand, which Torrence mechanically supplied with a packet of tobacco.

'For my part,' Maigret said eventually, 'I saw Pietr, or

whoever has taken over his role, check in at Hôtel Majestic and have dinner with the Mortimer-Levingstons, which seems to have been arranged in advance.'

'The millionaires?'

'Yes, that's right. After the meal, Pietr went back to his suite. I warned the American. Mortimer then went to his room. They were obviously planning to go out as a three-some, since Mrs Mortimer came down straight after, in full evening gear. Ten minutes later, both men had vanished. Our Latvian had switched his evening wear for less swanky clothes. He'd put on a cap, and the guard just assumed he was a kitchen worker. But Levingston left as he was, in formal attire.'

Torrence said nothing. In the long pause that ensued, you could hear the fire roaring in the stove and the window panes rattling in the storm.

Torrence finally broke the silence.

'Luggage?' he asked.

'Done. Nothing there! Just clothes and underwear . . . The usual accoutrements of a first-class traveller. Not a scrap of paper. The Mortimer woman is certain that her husband has been murdered.'

Somewhere a bell rang. Maigret opened the drawer in his desk where that afternoon he'd put all the telegrams about Pietr the Latvian.

Then he looked at the map. He drew a line with his finger from Krakow to Bremen, then to Amsterdam, Brussels and Paris.

Somewhere near Saint-Quentin, a brief halt: a man died.

In Paris, the line came to a full stop. Two men vanish from the middle of the Champs-Élysées.

All that's left are suitcases in a suite and Mrs Mortimer-Levingston, whose mind is as empty as Pietr's travelling chest.

The gurgle from Maigret's pipe was getting so annoying that the inspector took a swatch of chicken feathers from another drawer, cleaned the shaft, then opened the stove door and flung the soiled feathers in the fire.

Four of the beer glasses were empty but for sticky froth marks on the rim. Somebody came out of one of the offices on the corridor, locked his door and went away.

'Who's a lucky man!' Torrence observed. 'That's Lucas. Tonight he got a tip-off from some moneyed brat and arrested a pair of drug dealers.'

Maigret was poking the fire, and when he stood up his face was crimson. In routine fashion he picked up the translucent paper, extracted the strand of hair and turned it over in the light. Then he went back to the map and studied the invisible track of Pietr's journey. It made a sweeping arc of almost 180 degrees.

If he had started out from Krakow, then why had he gone all the way north to Bremen before swerving back down to Paris?

He was still holding the slip of paper. He muttered:

'There must have been a picture inside this once.'

In fact, the tissue was a glassine envelope, a slipcover of the kind photographers use to protect customers' orders. But it was an obsolete size known as 'album format' that could only now be found in provincial backwaters. The photo that this cover must have protected would have been about half the size of a standard postcard, printed on off-white glacé paper on cardboard backing.

'Is anyone still there at the lab?' Maigret suddenly asked.

'I guess so. They must still be processing the photos of the Étoile du Nord affair.'

There was only one full glass left on the table. Maigret gulped it down and put on his jacket.

'You'll come along? . . . Those kinds of portrait photos usually have the name and address of the photographer printed or embossed on them . . .'

Torrence got the point. They set off through a labyrinth of passageways and stairs up into the attic floors of the Law Courts and finally found the forensics lab.

An expert took the slipcover, ran it through his fingers, almost sniffed at it. Then he sat at an arc lamp and wheeled over a carriage-mounted multiplying glass.

The principle is straightforward: blank paper that has been in protracted contact with another sheet that has been printed or written on eventually acquires an imprint of the letters on that other sheet. The imprint cannot be seen by the naked eye, but photography can reveal it.

The fact that there was a stove in the lab meant that Maigret was destined to end up there. He stood watch for the best part of an hour, smoking pipe after pipe, while Torrence trailed the photographer as he came and went.

At long last the darkroom door opened. A voice cried out:

'We've got it!'

'Yes?'

'The photo credit is: *Léon Moutet, Art Photography, Quai des Belges, Fécamp.*'

Only a real expert could decipher the plate. Torrence, for instance, could only see a blur.

'Do you want to see the post-mortem photos?' the

expert asked cheerfully. 'They're first-rate! But it was a tight fit inside that railway toilet! Would you believe it, we had to hang the camera from the ceiling . . .'

'Have you got an outside line?' Maigret asked, gesturing towards the phone.

'Yes . . . the switchboard shuts down at nine, so before she goes off the operator connects me to the outside.'

Maigret called the Majestic and spoke to one of the desk interpreters.

'Has Mr Mortimer-Levingston come back in?'

'I'll find out for you, sir. To whom do I have the honour of . . .'

'Police!'

'No, sir, he's not back.'

'What about Mr Oswald Oppenheim?'

'Not back either, sir.'

'What is Mrs Mortimer up to?'

A pause.

'I asked you what Mrs Mortimer is doing.'

'She is . . . I think she is in the bar . . .'

'Do you mean she's drunk?'

'She has had a few cocktails, sir. She said she would not go up to her suite until her husband comes back . . . Do you . . . ?'

'What's that?'

'Hello? . . . This is the manager speaking,' another voice broke in. 'Any progress? Do you think this will get into the papers? . . .'

Cruelly, Maigret hung up. To please the photographer he took a look at the first proof photos laid out in the drying trays, still gleaming wet. While doing that he was talking to Torrence.

'You're going to settle in at the Majestic, old pal. The main thing is to take no notice whatsoever of the manager.'

'What about you, *patron*?'

'I'm going back to the office. There's a train to Fécamp at 5.30, It's not worth going home and waking up Mme Maigret. Hang on . . . The Dauphine should still be open. On your way, order me up a beer . . .'

'Just one . . . ?' Torrence inquired, with a deadpan expression on his face.

'As you like, old pal! The waiter's smart enough to know it means three or four. Have him throw in a few sandwiches as well.'

They traipsed down an unending spiral staircase in single file.

The black-gowned photographer was left on his own to admire the prints he'd just made. He still had to number them.

The two detectives parted company in the freezing courtyard.

'If you leave the Majestic for any reason, make sure one of our men holds the fort,' Maigret instructed. 'I'll telephone the front desk if I need to get in touch . . .'

He went back to his office and stoked the fire so vigorously he could have snapped the grate.

4. *The Seeteufel's First Mate*

The station at La Bréauté, on the main line to Le Havre, where Maigret had to change trains at 7.30 a.m., gave him a foretaste of Fécamp.

The ill-lit station buffet had grimy walls and a counter offering only a few mouldy pieces of cake alongside a miserable fruit stack made of three bananas and five oranges.

The foul weather had even more impact here than in Paris. Rain was coming down in buckets. Crossing from one track to the other meant wading through knee-deep mud.

The branch-line train was a rickety affair made up of carriages on their way to scrap. In the pale half-light of dawn you could hardly make out the fuzzy shapes of farmhouses through the pelting rain.

Fécamp! The air was laden with the smell of herring and cod. Mountains of casks. Ships' masts peering over the locomotive. Somewhere a siren blared.

'Quai des Belges?'

Straight ahead. All he had to do was walk through slimy puddles gleaming with fish scales and rotting innards.

The photographer was also a shopkeeper and a newspaper vendor. He stocked oilskins, sailcloth pea-jackets and hempen rope alongside New Year's greeting cards.

A weakling with very pale skin: as soon as he heard the word 'police' he called his wife to the rescue.

'Can you tell me what photo was in this slipcover?'

It dragged on. Maigret had to squeeze words out of him one by one and do his thinking for him.

In the first place, the technician hadn't used that format for eight years, ever since he'd acquired new equipment to do postcard-sized portraits.

Who might have had his or her photograph taken eight or more years ago? Monsieur Moutet took a whole fifteen minutes to remember that he'd got an album with archive copies of all the portraits done in his establishment.

His wife went to get it. Sailors came and went. Kids came in to buy a penny's worth of sweets. Outside, ships' tackle scraped on the dock. You could hear the waves shifting shingle along the breakwater.

Maigret thumbed through the archive album, then specified what he was looking for:

'A young woman with extremely fine brown hair . . .'

That did it.

'Mademoiselle Swaan!' the photographer exclaimed. He turned up the snapshot straight away. It was the only time he'd had a decent subject to photograph.

She was a pretty woman. She looked twenty. The photo fitted the slipcover exactly.

'Who is she?'

'She's still living in Fécamp. But now she's got a clifftop villa five minutes from the Casino . . .'

'Is she married?'

'She wasn't then. She was the cashier at the Railway Hotel.'

'Opposite the station, I suppose?'

'Yes, you must have seen it on your way here. She was an orphan from some small place around here . . . Les Loges . . . Do you know where I mean? . . . Anyway, that's

how she got to meet a traveller staying at the hotel . . .
They got married . . . At the moment she's living in the
villa with her two children and a maid . . .'

'Mr Swaan doesn't live in Fécamp?'

There was a pause. The photographer and his wife
exchanged glances. The woman answered:

'Since you're from the police, I suppose we'd better tell
you everything. Anyway you'd find it all out in the end,
but . . . They're only rumours, but . . . Mr Swaan almost
never stays in Fécamp. When he does come he stops for a
few days at the most . . . Sometimes it's just a flying visit
. . . He first came not long after the war . . . The Grand
Banks were being reorganized, after five years' interrup-
tion. He wanted to look into it properly, so he said, and to
make investments in businesses that were being started
up again. He claimed to be Norwegian . . . His first name
is Olaf . . . The herring fishermen who sometimes go as
far as Norway say there are plenty of people over there
who have that name . . . Nonetheless, people said he was
really a German spy. That's why, when he got married, his
wife was kept at arm's length. Then we discovered he
really was a sailor and was first mate on a German mer-
chantman, and that was why he didn't show up very often
. . . Eventually people stopped bothering about him, but
we're still wary . . .'

'You said they had children?'

'Two . . . A little girl of three and a baby a few months
old . . .'

Maigret took the photograph out of the album and got
directions to the villa. It was a bit too early to turn up. He
waited in a harbour café for two hours, listening to fishermen talking about the herring catch, which was at its

height. Five trawlers were tied up at the quay. Fish was being unloaded by the barrelful. Despite the wind and rain, the air stank.

To get to the villa he walked along the deserted breakwater and around the shuttered Casino still plastered with last summer's posters. At last he got to a steep climb that began at the foot of the cliff. As he plodded up he got occasional glimpses of iron railings in front of villas. The one he was looking for turned out to be a comfortable-looking red-brick structure, neither large nor small. He guessed that the garden with its white-gravel paths was well tended in season. The windows must have had a good view into the far distance.

Maigret rang the bell. A great Dane came to sniff at him through the railings, and its lack of bark made it seem all the more ferocious. At the second ring, a maid appeared. First she took the dog back to his kennel, and then asked:

'What is it about?'

She spoke with the local accent.

'I would like to see Mr Swaan, please.'

She seemed hesitant.

'I don't know if sir is in . . . I'll go and ask.'

She hadn't opened the gate. Rain was still pouring down, and Maigret was soaked through. He watched the maid go up the steps and vanish inside the house. Then a curtain shifted at a window. A few moments later the maid reappeared.

'Sir will not be back for several weeks. He is in Bremen . . .'

'In that case I would like to have a word with Madame Swaan . . .'

The maid hesitated again, but ended up opening the gate.

'Madame isn't dressed. You will have to wait . . .'

The dripping detective was shown into a neat lounge with white curtains and a waxed floor. The furniture was brand new, but just the same as you would find in any lower-middle-class home. They were good-quality pieces, in a style that would have been called modern around 1900.

Light oak. Flowers in an 'artistic' stone vase in the middle of the table. Crochet-work place-mats. On the other hand, there was a magnificent sculpted silver samovar on a side-table. It must have been worth more than the rest of the room's contents put together.

Maigret heard noises coming from the first floor. A baby could be heard crying through one of the ground-floor walls; someone else was mumbling something in a soft and even voice, as if to comfort it. At last, the sound of slippered feet gliding along the corridor. The door opened. Maigret found himself facing a young woman who had dressed in a hurry so as to meet him.

She was of medium height, more plump than slim, with a pretty and serious face that betrayed a pang of anxiety. She smiled nonetheless and said:

'Why didn't you take a seat?'

Rivulets of rainwater flowed from Maigret's overcoat, trousers and shoes into little puddles on the polished floor. In that state he could not have sat down on the light-green velvet of the armchairs in the lounge.

'Madame Swaan, I presume? . . .'

'Yes, monsieur . . .'

She looked at him quizzically.

'I'm sorry to disturb you like this . . . It's just a formality

. . . I'm with the Immigration Service . . . We're conduct-
ing a survey . . .'

She said nothing. She didn't seem any more or less
anxious than before.

'I understand Mr Swaan is a Swede. Is that correct?'

'Oh no, he's Norwegian . . . But for the French I guess
it's the same thing . . . To begin with, I myself . . .'

'He is a ship's officer?'

'He's first mate on the *Seeteufel*, out of Bremen . . .'

'As I thought . . . So he is in the employ of a German
company?'

She blushed.

'The ship-owner is German, yes . . . At least, on paper . . .'

'Meaning? . . .'

'I don't think I need to keep it from you . . . You must
be aware that the merchant fleet has been in crisis since
the war . . . Even here you can find ocean-going captains
who've been unable to find commissions and who have
to take positions as first or even second mates . . . Others
have joined the Newfoundland or the North Sea fishing
fleets.'

She spoke quite fast, but in a gentle and even tone.

'My husband didn't want to take on a commission in
the Pacific, where there's more work, because he wouldn't
have been able to come back to Europe more than once
every two years . . . Shortly after we got married, some
Americans bought the *Seeteufel* in the name of a German
shipping firm . . . Olaf first came to Fécamp looking spe-
cifically for more schooners to buy . . . Now you must see
. . . The aim was to run booze to the USA . . . Substantial
firms were set up with American money . . . They have
offices in France, Holland, or Germany . . . The truth is

that my husband works for one of these companies. The *Seeteufel* sails what's called *Rum Alley*. It doesn't really have anything to do with Germany.'

'Is he at sea at the moment?' Maigret asked, keeping his eyes on that pretty face, which struck him as an honest and even at times a touching one.

'I don't think so. You must realize that the sailings aren't as regular as those of a liner. But I always try to keep abreast of the *Seeteufel*'s position. At the moment he ought to be in Bremen, or very nearly there.'

'Have you ever been to Norway?'

'Never! I've actually never left Normandy, so to speak. Just a couple of times, for short stays in Paris.'

'With your husband?'

'Yes . . . On our honeymoon, as well.'

'He's got fair hair, hasn't he?'

'Yes . . . Why do you ask?'

'And a thin, close-cropped blond moustache?'

'Yes . . . I can show you a picture of him if you like.'

She opened a door and went out. Maigret could hear her moving about in the bedroom next door.

She was out for longer than made sense, and the noises of doors opening and closing and of comings and goings around the house were just as illogical.

At last she came back, looking somewhat perplexed and apologetic.

'Please excuse me . . .' she said. 'I can't manage to put my hand on that photo . . . A house with children is always upside down . . .'

'One more question . . . To how many people did you give a copy of this photograph of yourself?'

Maigret showed her the archive print he'd been given

by the photographer. Madame Swaan went bright red and stuttered:

'I don't understand . . .'

'Your husband presumably has one?'

'Yes . . . We were engaged when . . .'

'Does any other man have a print?'

She was on the verge of tears. The quiver of her lips gave away her distress.

'No, nobody.'

'Thank you, madame. That will be all.'

As he was leaving a little girl slipped into the hallway. Maigret had no need to memorize her features. She was the spitting image of Pietr the Latvian!

'Olga! . . .' her mother scolded, as she hustled her back through a half-open door.

Maigret was back outside in the rain and the wind.

'Goodbye, madame . . .'

He caught a final glimpse of her through the closing door. He was aware that he had left her at a loss, after bursting in on her in the warmth of her own home. He picked up a trace in her eyes of something uncertain but undoubtedly akin to anxiety as she shut her front door.

5. The Russian Drunkard

You don't boast about these kinds of things, they would raise a laugh if they were mentioned out loud, but all the same, they call for a kind of heroism.

Maigret hadn't slept. From 5.30 to 8 a.m. he'd been shaken about in draughty railway carriages. Ever since he'd changed trains at La Bréauté he'd been soaked through. Now his shoes squelched out dirty water at every step and his bowler was a shapeless mess. His overcoat and trousers were sopping wet.

The wind was slapping him with more rain. The alleyway was deserted. It was no more than a steep path between garden walls. The middle of it had turned into a raging torrent.

He stood still for quite a while. Even his pipe had got wet in his pocket. There was no way of hiding near the villa. All he could do was stick as close as possible to a wall and wait.

Anyone coming by would catch sight of him and look round. He might have to stay there for hours on end. There was no definite proof that there was a man in the house. And even if he were there, why should he come out?

Grumpy as he was, Maigret filled his wet pipe with tobacco all the same, and wedged himself as best he could into a cranny in the wall . . .

This was no place for a detective chief inspector of the

Police Judiciaire. At most it was a job for a new recruit. Between the age of twenty-two and thirty he'd stood this sort of watch a hundred times over.

He had a terrible time getting a match to light. The emery board on the side of the box was coming off in strips. If one of the sticks hadn't finally ignited, maybe even Maigret would have given up and gone home.

He couldn't see anything from where he was standing except a low wall and the green-painted railing of the villa. He had brambles at his ankles and a draught all down his neck.

Fécamp was laid out beneath him, but he could not see the town. He could only hear the roar of the sea and now and again a siren or the sound of a car.

After half an hour on watch he saw a woman with a shopping basket, who looked like a cook, making her way up the steep slope. She only saw Maigret when she passed close by him. His huge, unmoving shape standing next to the wall in a wind-swept alley so scared her that she started to run.

Perhaps she worked for one of the villas at the top of the rise? A few minutes later a man appeared at the bend and stared at Maigret from afar. Then a woman joined him, and both went back inside.

It was a ridiculous situation. The inspector knew there wasn't one chance in ten that his surveillance would be of any use.

Yet he stuck it out – just because of a vague feeling that didn't even deserve to be called an intuition. In fact it was a pet theory of his that he'd never worked out in full and remained vague in his mind, but which he dubbed for his own use *the theory of the crack in the wall*.

Inside every wrong-doer and crook there lives a human being. In addition, of course, there is an opponent in a game, and it's the player that the police are inclined to see. As a rule, that's what they go after.

Some crime or offence is committed. The match starts on the basis of more or less objective facts. It's a problem with one or more unknowns that a rational mind tries to solve.

Maigret worked like any other policeman. Like everyone else, he used the amazing tools that men like Bertillon, Reiss and Locard have given the police – anthropometry, the principle of the trace, and so forth – and that have turned detection into forensic science. But what he sought, what he waited and watched out for, was the *crack in the wall*. In other words, the instant when the human being comes out from behind the opponent.

At the Majestic he'd seen the player. But here, he had a premonition of something else. The tidy, quiet villa wasn't one of the props that Pietr used to play his hand. Especially the wife and the children he'd seen and heard: they belonged to a different physical and moral order.

That's why he was waiting, albeit in a foul mood, for he was too fond of his big cast-iron stove and his office with glasses of frothy beer on the table not to be miserable in such awful weather.

He'd started his watch a little after 10.30. At half past noon he heard footsteps scrunching the gravel and swift, practised movements opening the gate, which brought a figure to within three metres of the inspector. The lie of the land made it impossible for Maigret to retreat. So he stood his ground unwaveringly, or, to be more precise, inertly, standing on two legs that could be seen in the round through the sopping wet trousers that clung to them.

The man leaving the villa was wearing a poor-quality belted trenchcoat, with its worn-out collar upturned. He was also wearing a grey cap. The get-up made him look very young. He went down the hill with his hands in his pockets, all hunched up and shivering because of the contrast in temperature.

He was obliged to pass within a metre of the Detective Chief Inspector. He chose that moment to slow down, take a packet of cigarettes out of his pocket and light up. It was as if he'd positively tried to get his face into the light so as to allow the detective to study it in detail!

Maigret let him go on a few paces, then set off on his tail, with a frown on his face. His pipe had gone out. His whole being exuded a sense of displeasure as well as an ardent desire to understand.

The man in the trenchcoat looked like the Latvian and yet did not resemble him! Same height: about 1 m 68cm. At a pinch he could be the same age, though in the outfit he was wearing he looked closer to twenty-six than thirty-two. There was nothing to determine that this man was not the original of the 'word-picture' that Maigret knew by heart and also had on a piece of paper in his pocket.

And yet . . . it was not the same man! For one thing, his eyes had a vaguer, more sentimental expression. They were a lighter shade of grey, as if the rain had scrubbed them. Nor did he have a blond toothbrush moustache. But that wasn't the only thing that made him different.

Maigret was struck by other details. His outfit was nothing like that of an officer of the merchant fleet. It didn't even fit the villa, given the comfortable middle-class style of living that it implied.

His shoes were worn and the heels had been redone. Because of the mud, the man hitched up his trouser legs, showing faded grey cotton socks that had been clumsily darned.

There were lots of stains on the trenchcoat. Overall, the man fitted a type that Maigret knew well: the migrant low-lifer, predominantly of Eastern European origin, who slept in squalid lodging houses and sometimes in railway stations. A type not often seen outside Paris, but accustomed to travelling in third-class carriages when not riding the footboards or hopping freight trains.

He got proof of his insight a few minutes later. Fécamp doesn't have any genuine low dives, but behind the harbour there are two or three squalid bars favoured by dockhands and seamen. Ten metres before these places there's a regular café kept clean and bright. The man in the trenchcoat walked right past it and straight into the least prepossessing of the bars, where he put his elbow on the counter in a way that Maigret saw right through.

It was the straightforwardly vulgar body-language of a guttersnipe. Even if he'd tried, Maigret couldn't have imitated it. The inspector followed the man into the bar. He'd ordered an absinthe substitute and was just standing there, wordless, with a blank stare on his face. He didn't register Maigret's presence, though the inspector was now right next to him.

Through a gap in the man's jacket Maigret could see that his linen was dirty. That's not something that can be simulated, either! His shirt and collar – now not much more than a ribbon – had been worn for days, maybe for weeks on end. They'd been slept in – God knows where! They'd been sweated in and rained on.

The man's suit was not unstylish, but it bore the same signs and told the same miserable story of a vagrant life.

'Same again!'

The glass was empty, and the barman refilled it, serving Maigret a measure of spirits at the same time.

'So you're back in these parts again? . . .'

The man didn't answer. He downed his drink in one gulp and gestured for a refill straight away.

'Anything to eat? . . . I've got some pickled herring . . .'

Maigret had sidled up to a small stove, and stood in front of it to warm his back, now as shiny as an umbrella.

'Come to think of it . . . I had a man in here last week from your part of the world . . . Russian he was, from Archangelsk . . . Sailing a Swedish three-master that had to put in to port because of the bad weather . . . Hardly had time to drink his fill, I can tell you! . . . Had a devil of a job on his hands . . . Torn sails, snapped yards, you name it . . .'

The man, now on his fourth imitation absinthe, was drinking steadily. The barman filled his glass every time it was empty, glancing at Maigret with a conniving wink.

'As for Captain Swaan, I ain't seen him since you was here last.'

Maigret shuddered. The man in the trenchcoat who'd now downed his fifth neat ersatz absinthe staggered towards the stove, bumped into the detective and held out his hands towards the warmth.

'I'll have a herring, all the same . . .' he said.

He had a quite strong accent – a Russian accent, as far as the detective could judge.

There they were, next to each other, shoulder to shoulder, so to speak. The man wiped his face with his hand several times, and his eyes grew ever more murky.

'Where's my glass? . . .' he inquired testily.

It had to be put in his hand. As he drank he stared at Maigret and pouted with disgust.

There was no mistaking that expression! As if to assert his opinion all the more clearly, he threw his glass to the ground, leaned on the back of a chair and muttered something in a foreign tongue.

The barman, somewhat concerned, found a way of getting close to Maigret and whispering quietly in a way that was nonetheless audible to the Russian:

'Don't take any notice of him. He's always like that . . .'

The man gave a drunkard's strangled laugh. He slumped into the chair, put his head in both his hands and stayed like that until a plate of herring was pushed over the table between his elbows. The barman shook his shoulder.

'Eat up! . . . It'll do you good . . .'

The man laughed again. It was more like a bitter cough. He turned round so he could see Maigret and stare at him aggressively, then he pushed the plate of herring off the table.

'More drink! . . .'

The barman raised his arms and grunted as if it was an excuse:

'Russians, I ask you!'

Then he put his finger to his head and turned it, as if he was tightening a loose screw.

★

Maigret had pushed his bowler to the back of his head. His clothes were steaming, giving off a grey haze. He was only up to his second glass of spirits.

'I'll have some herring!' he said.

He was still eating it with a slice of bread when the Russian got up on unsteady legs, looked around as if he didn't know what to do and grinned for the third time when he set eyes on Maigret.

Then he slumped down at the bar, took a glass from the shelf and a bottle from the enamel sink where it was being kept cool in water. He helped himself without watching how much he was taking and smacked his tongue as he drank.

Eventually he took a 100 franc note out of his pocket.

'Is that enough, you swine?' he asked the waiter.

He threw the banknote up in the air. The barman had to fish it out of the sink.

The Russian struggled with the door handle, which wouldn't open. There was almost a fight because the barman tried to help his customer, who kept elbowing him away.

At long last the trenchcoat faded away into the mist and rain along the harbour-side, going towards the station.

'That's an odd 'un,' the barman sighed, intending to be heard by Maigret, who was paying his bill.

'Is he often in?'

'Now and again . . . Once he spent the whole night here, on the bench where you're sitting . . . He's a real Russian! . . . Some Russian sailors who were here in Fécamp at the same time as he was told me so . . . Apparently he's quite educated . . . Did you look at his hands? . . .'

'Don't you think he's got the same looks as Captain Swaan? . . .'

'Oh! So you know him . . . Well, of course he does! But not so much as you'd mistake one for the other . . . All the same . . . For ages I thought it was his brother.'

The beige silhouette vanished round a corner. Maigret started to walk faster. He caught up with the Russian just as he was going into the third-class waiting room at the station. The man slumped onto a bench and once again put his head in his hands.

An hour later they were in the same railway compartment with a cattle trader from Yvetot who launched into shaggy-dog stories in Norman dialect. Now and again he nudged Maigret to draw his attention to the other passenger.

The Russian slipped down little by little and ended up in a crumpled heap on the bench. His face was pale, his chin was on his chest, and his half-open mouth stank of cheap spirits.

6. *Au Roi de Sicile*

The Russian woke up at La Bréauté and stayed awake from then on. It has to be said that the express from Le Havre to Paris was completely packed. Maigret and his travelling companion had to stand in the corridor, stuck near a door, watching random scenery fly by as the darkness swallowed it bit by bit.

The man in the trenchcoat seemed entirely unflustered at having a detective by his side. On arrival at Gare Saint-Lazare, he didn't try to use the milling crowd to throw Maigret off his tail. On the contrary: he went down the great staircase in leisurely fashion, realized that his packet of cigarettes was wet through, bought another one at a station stall and was on the verge of going into a bar. Then he changed his mind and began to loiter along the pavement. He made a sorry sight: a man so absent from the world and in such low spirits that he was no longer capable of reacting to anything.

It's a long way from Gare Saint-Lazare to Hôtel de Ville, there's the whole city centre to get through. Between six and seven in the evening, pedestrians flood the pavements in ocean waves, and traffic pulses along the streets like blood pumping down an artery.

With his mud- and grease-stained coat belted at the waist and his recycled heels, the narrow-shouldered pauper

45

waded on through the bright lights and the bustle. People elbowed and bumped into him, but he never stopped or looked over his shoulder.

He took the shortest route, by way of Rue du 4-Septembre and then through Les Halles, which proved he'd gone this way before.

He reached the ghetto of Paris, that's to say, the area around Rue des Rosiers, in the Marais. He sidled past shop fronts with signs in Yiddish, kosher butchers and window displays of *matzot*. At one corner, giving on to a passageway so dark and deep it looked like a tunnel, a woman tried to take him by the arm, but let go without his saying a word. Presumably he had made a strong impression on her.

At last he ended up in Rue du Roi-de-Sicile, a winding street giving on to dead-end alleys, narrow lanes and overpopulated courtyards – a half-Jewish, half-Polish colony. Two hundred metres along, he dived into a hotel entrance.

The hotel's name, Au Roi de Sicile, was written out on ceramic tiles. Underneath the nameplate were notices in Yiddish, Polish, maybe also Russian and other suchlike languages that Maigret didn't know.

There was a building site next door where the remains of a house that had needed buttressing to keep it standing were still visible. It was still raining, but in this rat-trap there was no wind.

Maigret heard a window closing with a sharp clack on the third floor of the hotel. No less resolutely than the Russian, he went inside.

There was no door in the entrance hall, just a staircase

. . . At the mezzanine level there was a kind of glass box where a Jewish family was having dinner.

Inspector Maigret knocked, but instead of opening the door the concierge raised a hatch, like at a ticket counter. A rancid smell wafted from it. The man was wearing a skullcap. His overweight wife carried on with her meal.

'What is it?'

'Police! Give me the name of the tenant who just came in.'

The man grunted something in his own language, then went to a drawer and brought out a grimy ledger that he shoved through the hatch without a word.

At the same instant Maigret sensed he was being watched from the unlit stairwell. He turned round quickly and saw an eye shining from about ten stairs above.

'Room number?'

'Thirty-two . . .'

He thumbed through the ledger and read:

Fyodor Yurevich, age 28, born Vilna, labourer, and Anna Gorskin, age 25, born Odessa, no occupation.

The Jew had gone back to the table to continue eating his meal like a man without a worry. Maigret drummed on the window. The hotel-keeper stood up slowly and reluctantly.

'How long has he been staying here?'

'About three years.'

'What about Anna Gorskin?'

'She's been here longer than he has . . . Maybe four and a half years . . .'

'What do they live on?'

'You've read the book . . . He's a labourer.'

'Don't try that on me!' Maigret riposted in a voice that sufficed to change the hotelier's attitude.

'It's not for me to stick my nose in where it's not wanted, is it?' he now said in an oilier tone. 'He pays up on time. He comes and he goes and it's not my job to follow him around . . .'

'Does anybody come to see him?'

'Sometimes . . . I've got over sixty tenants in here and I can't keep an eye on all of them at once . . . As long as they're doing no harm! . . . Anyway, as you're from the police you should know all about this establishment . . . I make proper returns . . . Officer Vermouillet can confirm that . . . He's the one who comes every week . . .'

Maigret turned around on an impulse and called out:

'Anna Gorskin, come down now!'

There was a ruffling noise in the stairway, then the sound of footsteps, and finally a woman stepped out into a patch of light.

She looked older than the ledger's claim of twenty-five. That was probably hereditary. Like many Jewish women of her age, she had put on weight, but she was still quite good-looking. She had remarkable eyes: very dark pupils set in amazingly white and shining corneas. But the rest of her was so sloppy as to spoil that first impression. Her black, greasy and uncombed hair fell in thick bunches onto her neck. She was wearing a worn-out dressing gown, loosely tied and allowing a glimpse of her underwear. Her stockings were rolled down above her thick knees.

'What were you doing in the stairwell?'

'I live here, don't I? . . .'

Maigret sensed straight away what kind of a woman

he was dealing with. Excitable, irreverent, hammer and tongs. At the drop of a hat she could throw a fit, rouse the entire building, give an ear-splitting scream and probably accuse him of outlandish offences. Did she perhaps know she was unassailable? In any case, she looked at her enemy with defiance.

'You'd be better advised to go look after your man . . .'

'None of your business . . .'

The hotelier stayed behind his window, rocking his head from left to right, from right to left, with a morose and reproving look on his face; but there was laughter in his eyes.

'When did Fyodor leave?'

'Yesterday evening . . . At eleven . . .'

She was lying! Plain as day! But there was no point coming at her head-on – unless he wanted to pin back her arms and march her down to the station.

'Where does he work?'

'Wherever he chooses . . .'

You could see her breasts heave under her ill-fitting dressing gown. There was a hostile, haughty sneer on her face.

'What've the police got against Fyodor, anyway?'

Maigret decided to say rather quietly:

'Get upstairs . . .'

'I'll go when I feel like it! You ain't got no right to order me about.'

What was the point of answering back and risking creating an ugly incident that would only hold things up? Maigret shut the ledger and handed it back to the hotel-keeper.

'All above board and hunky-dory, right?' the latter said, after gesturing at the young woman to keep quiet. But she stood her ground with her fists on her hips, one side of her lit by the light from the hotelier's office, the other in darkness.

Maigret looked at her again. She met his gaze straight on and felt the need to mutter:

'You don't scare me one bit . . .'

He just shrugged and then made his way down a staircase so narrow his shoulders touched both of its squalid walls.

In the corridor he ran into two bare-necked Poles who turned away as soon as they saw him. The street was wet, making the cobblestones glint. In every corner, in the smallest pools of shadow, in the back alleys and passage- ways you could sense a swarm of humiliated and rebellious humanity. Shadowy figures flitted past. Shopkeepers sold products whose very names were unknown in France.

Less than 100 metres away was Rue de Rivoli and Rue Saint-Antoine – broad, well-lit streets with trams, market stalls and the city police . . . Maigret caught a passing street urchin with a cauliflower ear by the shoulder:

'Go fetch me a policeman from Place Saint-Paul . . .'

But the lad just looked at him with fear in his eyes, then answered in some incomprehensible tongue. He didn't know a word of French!

The inspector then spied a beggar.

'Here's a five franc coin . . . Take this note to the cop at Place Saint-Paul.'

The tramp understood. Ten minutes later a uniformed sergeant turned up.

'Call the Police Judiciaire and tell them to send me an officer straight away . . . Dufour, if he's free . . .'

Maigret cooled his heels for at least another half-hour. People went into the hotel. Others came out. But the light stayed on at the third-floor window, second from the left.

Anna Gorskin appeared at the doorway. She'd put on a greenish overcoat over her dressing gown. She was hatless and despite the rain she was wearing red satin sandals. She splashed her way across the street. Maigret kept out of sight, in the shadows.

She went into a store and came out a few minutes later laden with a host of small white packets, plus two bottles. She vanished back into the hotel.

At long last Inspector Dufour showed up. He was thirty-five and spoke three languages quite fluently, which made him a precious asset. But he had a habit of making the simplest things sound complicated. He could turn a common burglary or a banal snatch-and-grab case into a dramatic mystery, tying himself up in knots of his own making. But as he was also uncommonly persistent, he was highly suitable for a well-defined job like staking out or tailing a suspect.

Maigret gave him a description of Fyodor Yurevich and his girlfriend.

'I'll send you a back-up. If one of those two comes out, stay on their tail. But one of you has to stay behind to man the stake-out . . . Got that?'

'Are we still on the Étoile du Nord case? . . . It's a mafia hit, right?'

Maigret went off without answering. He got to his office at Quai des Orfèvres fifteen minutes later, dispatched an officer to back up Dufour, leaned over his stove and swore at Jean for not stoking it up to a red-hot glow. He hung his sopping greatcoat on the back of the door. It had gone so stiff that the shape of his shoulders could still be made out in it.

'Did my wife call?'

'This morning . . . She was told you were out on a case . . .'

She was used to that. He knew that if he went home she would just give him a kiss, stir the pot on the stove and serve him a delicious plate of stew. The most she would dare – but only when he'd sat down to eat – would be to put her chin on her hand and ask:

'Everything OK? . . .'

The meal would always be ready for him, whether he turned up at noon or at five.

'Torrence?' he asked Jean.

'He called at 7 a.m.'

'From the Majestic?'

'I don't know. He asked if you'd left.'

'What else?'

'He called again at ten past five this afternoon. He asked for you to be told he was waiting for you.'

Maigret had only had a herring to eat since the morning. He stayed upright in front of his stove for a while. It was beginning to roar, for Maigret had an unrivalled knack for getting even the least combustible coal to catch. Then he plodded his way to the cupboard, where there was an enamel sink, a towel, a mirror and a suitcase. He dragged the case into the middle of his office, undressed and put on clean underwear and dry clothes. He rubbed his unshaven chin.

'It'll have to do . . .'

He looked lovingly at the fire, which was now burning

grandly, placed two chairs next to it and carefully laid out his wet clothes on them. There was one sandwich left over from the previous night on his desk, and he wolfed it down, still standing, ready to depart. Only there wasn't any beer. He was more than a little parched.

'If anything at all comes in for me, I'm at the Majestic,' he said to Jean. 'Get them to call me.'

And at long last he slumped into the back seat of a taxi.

7. The Third Interval

Torrence wasn't to be found in the lobby, but in a first-floor room in front of a top-notch dinner. He explained with a broad wink:

'It's all the manager's fault! . . . He practically went down on bended knee to get me to accept this room and the gourmet meals he sends up . . .'

He was speaking in a whisper. He pointed to a door.

'The Mortimers are next door . . .'

'Mortimer came back?'

'Around six this morning. In a foul mood. Wet, dirty, with chalk or lime all over his clothes . . .'

'What did he say?'

'Nothing . . . He tried to get back to his room without being noticed. But they told him his wife had waited up for him in the bar. And she had! . . . She'd ended up befriending a Brazilian couple . . . They had to keep the bar open all night just for them . . . She was atrociously drunk . . .'

'And then?'

'He went as white as a ghost. His mouth went all twisted. He said a curt hello to the Brazilians, then took his wife by the armpits and dragged her off without another word . . . I reckon she slept it off until four this afternoon . . . There wasn't a sound from their suite until then . . . Then I heard whispering . . . Mortimer rang the front desk to have the newspapers brought up . . .'

'Nothing about the case in the papers, I hope?'

'Not a word. They've respected the embargo. Just a two-liner saying that a corpse had been found on the Étoile du Nord and that the police were treating it as suicide.'

'Next?'

'Room service brought them up some lemon juice. Mortimer took a stroll around the lobby, went straight past me two or three times, looking worried. He sent coded wires to his New York bank and to his secretary, who's been in London these past few days . . .'

'That's it?'

'At the moment they're just finishing dinner. Oysters, cold chicken, salad. The hotel keeps me abreast of everything. The manager is so delighted to have me shut away up here that he'll sweat blood to do me any favour I ask. That's why he came up just now to tell me that the Mortimers have got tickets to see *The Epic* at the Gymnase Theatre tonight. A four-acter by someone or other . . .'

'Pietr's suite?'

'Quiet as the grave! Nobody has been in it. I locked the door and put a blob of wax on the keyhole, so nobody can get in without my knowing . . .'

Maigret had picked up a chicken leg and was chewing at it quite shamelessly while looking round for a stove that wasn't there. In the end he sat on the radiator and asked:

'Isn't there anything to drink?'

Torrence poured him a glass of a superb Mâcon blanc, which his chief drank thirstily. Then there was a scratching at the door and a valet entered in a conspiratorial manner.

'The manager requests me to inform you that Mr and Mrs Mortimer's car has been brought to the front.'

Maigret glanced at the table still laden with food with

the same sorrow he had expressed in his eyes on leaving the stove in his office.

'I'll go,' he said regretfully. 'You stay here.'

He tidied himself up in front of the mirror, wiping his mouth and his chin. A moment later he was in a taxi waiting for the Mortimer-Levingstons to get into their limousine.

They weren't long in coming. Mortimer was wearing a black overcoat that hid his dinner jacket; she was swaddled in furs, as on the previous night.

She must have still been tired, because her husband was discreetly propping her up with one hand. The limousine set off without a whisper.

Maigret hadn't known that this was an opening night at the Gymnase, and he was almost refused entry. City police formed a guard of honour beneath the canopy. In spite of the rain passers-by stopped to watch the guests alight from their cars. Inspector Maigret had to ask to see the manager and wait his turn in corridors, where he stuck out as the only person not wearing formal attire. The manager was at his wits' end, waving his arms about.

'There's nothing I'd like better than to oblige! But you're the twentieth person to ask me for a "spare seat"! There aren't any spare seats! There aren't any seats! . . . And you're not even properly dressed! . . .'

He was being assailed from all quarters.

'Can't you see? Put yourself in my shoes . . .'

In the end Maigret had to stay standing up next to a door with the usherettes and the programme-sellers.

The Mortimer-Levingstons had a box. There were six people in it, of whom one was a princess and another a government minister. People came and went. Hands were kissed, smiles exchanged.

The curtain rose on a sunlit garden. Shushes, murmurs, footsteps. Finally the actor's voice could be heard, wobbly at first but then more confident, creating an atmosphere.

Latecomers were still taking their seats. More shushing. Somewhere a woman giggled.

Mortimer was more lord of the manor than ever. Evening dress suited him to a tee. The white shirt-front brought out the ivory hue of his skin.

Did he see Maigret? Did he not? An usherette brought the inspector a stool to sit on, but he had to share it with a portly lady in black silk, the mother of one of the actresses.

First interval, second interval. Comings and goings in the boxes. Artificial enthusiasm. Greetings exchanged between the parterre and the circle. The foyer, the corridors and even the front steps buzzed like a hive in high summer. Names were dropped in a whisper – names of maharajahs, ministers, statesmen and artists.

Mortimer left his box on three occasions, reappearing in a stage-box and then in the pit, and finally to have a chat with a former prime minister, whose hearty laugh could be heard twenty rows away.

End of Act Three. Flowers on the stage. A skinny actress was given an ovation. Seats flapping up made a racket and shuffling feet sounded like the swell of the sea. When Maigret turned to look up at the Americans' box, Mortimer-Levingston had vanished.

Now for the fourth and last act. That was when anybody who had an excuse got into the wings and the actors' and actresses' dressing-rooms. Others besieged the cloak-rooms. There was much fussing over cars and taxis.

Maigret lost at least ten minutes looking around inside the theatre. Then, without hat or coat, he had to quiz the doorman and the policemen on duty outside to find out what he needed to know.

He learned eventually that the Mortimers' olive-green limousine had just driven off. He was shown where it had been parked, outside a bar often frequented by trad-ers in cloakroom receipts. The car had gone towards Porte Saint-Martin. The American plutocrat hadn't retrieved his overcoat.

Outside, clumps of theatre-goers huddled wherever they could get out of the rain.

Maigret smoked a pipe with his hands in his pockets and a grumpy look on his face. The bell rang. People flocked inside. Even the municipal police went in to watch the last act.

The Grands Boulevards looked as scruffy as they always did at 11 p.m. The shafts of rain lit by the streetlamps were thinning out. The audience spewed out of a cinema which then switched off its lighting, brought in its billboards, and shut its doors. People stood in line at a bus stop, beneath a green-striped lamp-post. When the bus came there was an argument, because there were no number-tags left in the ticket machine. A policeman got involved. Long after the bus had left he remained in contentious discussion with an indignant fat man.

At last a limousine came to a gliding halt on the tar-mac. The door opened even before it was at a standstill. Mortimer-Levingston, in tails but without a hat, bounded up the stairs and went into the warm and brightly lit lobby.

Maigret took a look at the chauffeur. He was 100 per cent American: he had a hard face with a jutting chin, and he sat stock still in his seat as if he'd been turned to stone by his uniform.

The inspetor opened one of the padded doors barely an inch or two. Mortimer was standing at the back of his box. A sarcastic actor was speaking his lines in staccato. Curtain. Flowers. Thunderous applause.

People rushing for the exits. More shushing. The lead actor uttered the name of the author and went to fetch him from a box to bring him centre stage. Mortimer kissed some hands and shook others, gave a 100 franc tip to the usherette who brought him their coats. His wife was pale-faced, with blue rings under her eyes. When they had got back into their car there was a moment of indecision.

The couple were having an argument. Mrs Levingston was agitated. Her husband lit a cigarette and put out his lighter with an angry swipe of his hand. Eventually, he said something to the chauffeur through the intercom tube, and the car set off, with Maigret in a taxi following behind.

It was half past midnight. Rue La Fayette. The white colonnade of La Trinité was sheathed in scaffolding. Rue de Clichy.

The limousine stopped in Rue Fontaine, outside Pickwick's Bar. A concierge in a blue and gold uniform. Coat check. A red curtain lifted and a snatch of tango emerged.

Maigret went in behind the couple and sat at a table near the door, which must have always stayed empty because it caught every draught.

The Mortimers had been seated near to the jazz band. The American read the menu and chose what he would have for supper. A professional dancer bowed to his wife. She went on the floor. Levingston watched her with remarkable intensity. She exchanged a few remarks with her dancing partner but never once turned towards the corner where Maigret was sitting.

Most people here were in formal attire, but there were also a few foreigners in lounge suits. Maigret waved away a hostess who tried to sit at his table. A bottle of champagne was put in front of him, automatically. There were streamers all about. Puffer balls flew through the air. One landed on Maigret's nose, and he glowered at the old lady who'd aimed it at him.

Mrs Mortimer had gone back to her table. The dancer wandered around the floor for a moment then went towards the exit and lit a cigarette. Suddenly he lifted the red plush curtain and vanished. It took three minutes for Maigret to think of going to see what was happening outside.

The dancer had gone.

The rest of the night dragged on drearily. The Mortimers ate copiously – caviar and truffles *au champagne*, then lobster *à l'américaine*, followed by cheese.

Mrs Mortimer didn't go back to the dance-floor.

Maigret didn't like champagne, but he sipped at it to slake his thirst. He made the mistake of nibbling the roasted almonds on the table, and that made him even thirstier.

He checked the time on his wristwatch: 2 a.m.

People began leaving the nightspot. Nobody took the slightest notice of a dancer performing her routine. A drunk foreigner with three women at his table was making more noise than all the other customers put together. The professional dancer, who had stayed outside for only fifteen minutes, had taken some other ladies round the dance-floor. But it was all over. Weariness had set in.

Mrs Mortimer looked worn out; her eyelids were dark blue.

Her husband signalled to an attendant. Fur coat, over-coat and top hat were brought.

Maigret sensed that the dancer, who was talking to the sax player, was watching him nervously.

He summoned the manager, who kept him waiting. He lost a few minutes.

When he finally got outside, the Americans' limousine was just going round the corner into Rue Notre-Dame-de-Lorette. There were half a dozen taxis waiting at the rank opposite. Maigret began crossing the road.

A gunshot rang out. Maigret put his hand to his chest, looked around, could not see anything, but heard the foot-steps of someone running away down Rue Pigalle.

He staggered on for a few metres, propelled by his own inertia. The concierge ran up to him and held him upright. People came out of Pickwick's Bar to see what was going on. Among them Maigret noticed the tense figure of the professional dancer.

8. *Maigret Gets Serious*

Taxi drivers who 'do nights' in Montmartre don't need things spelled out to them and often get the point without a word being said.

When the shot was fired, one of the waiting drivers at the rank opposite Pickwick's Bar was about to open the passenger door for Maigret, not knowing who he was. But maybe he guessed from the way the inspector held himself that he was about to give a ride to a cop.

Customers at a small bar on the opposite side of the street came running. Soon there would be a whole crowd gathered round the wounded man. In the blink of an eye the driver lent a hand to the doorman who was propping up Maigret, without a clue what else to do. In less than half a minute the taxi was on its way with the inspector in the back.

The car drove on for ten minutes or so and came to a halt in an empty street. The driver got out the front, opened the passenger door, and saw his customer sitting in an almost normal posture, with one hand under his jacket.

'I can see it's no big deal, like I thought. Where can I take you?'

Still, Maigret looked quite upset, mainly because it was a flesh wound. His chest had been torn; the bullet had grazed a rib and exited near his shoulder blade.

'Quai des Orfèvres . . .'

The driver muttered something that couldn't be made out. En route, the inspector changed his mind.

'Take me to Hôtel Majestic . . . Drop me off at the service entrance on Rue de Ponthieu . . .'

He screwed up his handkerchief into a ball and stuffed it over his wound. He noted that the bleeding had stopped.

As he progressed towards the heart of Paris he appeared to be in less pain, but increasingly worried.

The taxi-driver tried to help him out. Maigret brushed him off and crossed the pavement with a steady gait. In a narrow entranceway he found the watchman drowsing behind his counter.

'Anything happen?'

'What do you mean?'

It was cold. Maigret went back out to pay the driver, who grunted once again because all he was getting for his great exploit was a measly 100 franc tip.

In the state he was in, Maigret was an impressive sight. He was still pressing his handkerchief to his chest wound, under his jacket. He held one shoulder higher than the other, but all the same he was being careful to save his strength. He was slightly light-headed. Now and again he felt as if he was floating on air, and he had to make an effort to get a grip on himself so as to see clearly and move normally.

He climbed an iron stairway that led to the upper floors, opened a door, found he was in a corridor, got lost in the labyrinth and came upon another stairway identical to the first, except that it had a different number on it.

He was going round in circles in the hotel's back passages. Luckily he came across a chef in a white toque, who stared at him in fright.

'Take me to the first floor . . . Room next to the Mortimers' suite.'

In the first place, however, the chef wasn't privy to the names of the hotel guests. In the second place, he was awed by the five blood streaks that Maigret had put on his face when he'd wiped it with his hand. He was struck dumb by this giant of a man lost in a narrow servants' corridor with his coat worn over his shoulders and his hand permanently stuck to his chest, distorting the shape of his waistcoat and jacket.

'Police!'

Maigret was running out of patience.

He felt the threat of a dizzy spell coming on. His wound was burning hot and prickling, as if long needles were going through it.

At long last the chef set off without looking over his shoulder. Soon Maigret felt carpet beneath his feet, and he realized he'd left the service area and was in the hotel proper. He kept an eye on the room numbers. He was on the odd-numbered side.

Eventually he came across a terrified valet.

'The Mortimers' suite?'

'Downstairs . . . But . . . You . . .'

He went down a stairway, and meanwhile, the news spread among the staff that there was a strange wounded man wandering about the hotel like a ghost.

Maigret stopped to rest against a wall for a moment and left a bloodstain on it; three very dark red drops also fell on the carpet.

At last he caught sight of the Mortimers' suite and, beside it, the door of the room where Torrence was to be found. He got to the door, walking slightly crabwise, pushed it open . . .

'Torrence! . . .'

The lights were on. The table was still laden with food and drink. Maigret's thick eyebrows puckered. He could not see his partner. On the other hand he could smell something in the air that reminded him of a hospital.

He took a few more wobbly steps. And suddenly came to a stop by a settee.

A black-leather-shod foot was sticking out from under it.

He had to try three times over. As soon as he took his hand off his wound, blood spurted out of it at an alarming rate. Finally he took the towel that was lying on the table and wedged it under his waistcoat, which he fastened as tight as he could. The smell in the room made him nauseous.

He lifted one end of the settee with weak arms and swung it round on two of its legs. It was what he expected: Torrence, all crumpled up, with his shoulder twisted round as if he'd had his bones broken to make him fit into a small space.

There was a bandage over the lower part of his face, but it wasn't knotted. Maigret got down on his knees.

Every gesture was measured and even slow – no doubt because of the state he was in. His hand hovered over Torrence's chest before daring to feel for his heart. When it reached its target, Maigret froze. He didn't stir but stayed kneeling on the carpet and stared at his partner.

Torrence was dead! Involuntarily Maigret twisted his lips and clenched his fist. His eyes clouded over and he uttered a terrible oath in the shut and silent room.

It could have sounded merely grotesque. But it did not! It was fearsome! Tragic! Terrifying!

Maigret's face had hardened. He didn't cry. That must be something he was unable to do. But his expression was full of such anger and pain as well as astonishment that it came close to looking stunned.

Torrence was thirty years old. For the last five years he had worked pretty much exclusively for Inspector Maigret.

His mouth was wide open, as if he'd made a desperate attempt at getting his last gasp of air.

One floor up, a traveller was taking off his shoes, directly over the dead man's body.

Maigret looked around to seek out the enemy. He was breathing heavily.

Several minutes passed in this manner. Maigret got up only when he sensed some hidden process beginning to work inside him.

He went to the window, opened it and looked out on the empty roadway of the Champs-Élysées. He let the breeze cool his brow then went to pick up the gag he'd ripped off Torrence's mouth.

It was a damask table napkin embroidered with the monogram of the Majestic. It still gave off a faint whiff of chloroform. Maigret stayed upright. His mind was a blank, with just a few shapeless thoughts knocking about inside it and raising painful associations.

Once again, as he had done in the hotel passageway, he leaned his shoulder on the wall, and quite suddenly his features seemed to sink. He had aged; his spirits were low. Was he at that moment in time on the verge of bursting into tears? No, he was too big and substantial. He was made of a tougher cloth.

The settee was squint and touching the table that hadn't

been cleared. On one plate chicken bones were mixed up with cigarette butts.

The inspector stretched out an arm towards the telephone. But he didn't pick up the receiver. Instead, he snapped his fingers in anger, turned back towards the corpse and stared at it.

He scowled bitterly and ironically when he thought of all the regulations, formal procedures and precautions he had to observe to please the examining magistrate.

Did any of that matter? It was Torrence, for heaven's sake! Almost the same as if it had been himself, dammit!

Torrence, who was part of the team, who . . .

Despite his apparent calm he unbuttoned his colleague's waistcoat with such feverish energy that he snapped off two of its buttons. That's when he saw something that made his face go quite grey.

On Torrence's shirt, *exactly over the centre of his heart*, there was a small brown mark.

Smaller than a chickpea! There was just one single drop of blood, and it had coagulated into a clot no larger than a pinhead. Maigret's eyes clouded over, and he twisted his face into a grimace of outrage he could not express in words.

It was disgusting, but in terms of crime it was the very apex of skill! He need look no further. He knew what the trick was, because he'd learned about it a few months earlier, in an article in a German crime studies journal.

First the chloroform towel, which overpowers the victim in twenty to thirty seconds. Then the long needle. The murderer can take his time and find just the right place between the ribs to get it straight into the heart, taking a life without any noise or mess.

Exactly the same method had been used in Hamburg six months earlier.

A bullet can miss its targets or just wound a man – Maigret was living proof of that. But a needle plunged into the heart of a man already made inert kills him scientifically, with no margin of error.

Inspector Maigret recalled one detail. That same evening, when the manager had reported that the Mortimers were leaving, he'd been sitting on the radiator, gnawing a chicken leg, and he'd been so overcome with his own comfort that he'd been on the verge of giving himself the hotel stake-out and sending Torrence to tail the millionaire at the theatre. That memory disturbed him. He felt awkward looking at his partner and felt nauseous, though he couldn't tell whether it was because of his wound, his emotions or the chloroform that was still hanging in the air.

It didn't even occur to him to start a proper methodical investigation.

It was Torrence lying there! Torrence, who'd been with him on all his cases these last few years! Torrence, a man who needed just one word, a single sign, to understand whatever he meant to say!

It was Torrence lying there with his mouth wide open as if he were still trying to suck in a bit of oxygen and keep on living! Maigret, who was unable to shed tears, felt sick and upset, with a weight on his shoulders, and nausea in his heart.

He went back to the telephone and spoke so quietly that he had to be asked to repeat his request.

'Police Judiciaire? . . . Yes . . . Hello! . . . Headquarters?

. . . Who is that speaking? . . . What? . . . Tarraud? . . . Listen, my lad . . . You're going to run round to the chief's address . . . Yes, his home address . . . Tell him . . . Tell him to join me at the Majestic . . . Straight away . . . Room . . . I don't know the room number, but he'll be shown up . . . What? . . . No, nothing else . . . .

'Hello? . . . What's that? . . . No, nothing wrong with me . . .'

He hung up. His colleague had started asking questions, puzzled by the odd sound of Maigret's voice, and also because what he'd asked for was odder still.

He stood there for a while longer, with his arms swinging by his side. He tried not to look at the corner of the room where Torrence lay. He caught sight of himself in a mirror and realized that blood had soaked through the towel. So, with great difficulty, he took off his jacket.

One hour later the Superintendent of Criminal Investigation knocked at the door. Maigret opened it a slit and grunted at the valet who'd brought up the chief to say he was no longer needed. He only opened the door further when the flunkey had vanished. Only then did the super realize that Maigret was bare-chested. The door to the bathroom was wide open, and the floor was a puddle of reddish water.

'Shut the door, sharpish,' Maigret said, with no regard for hierarchy.

On the right side of his chest was an elongated and now swollen flesh wound. His braces were hanging down his legs.

He nodded towards the corner of the room where Torrence was lying and put a finger to his lips.

'Shush! . . .'

The superintendent shuddered. In sudden agitation, he inquired:

'Is he dead?'

Maigret's chin fell to his chest.

'Could you give me a hand, chief?' he mumbled gloomily.

'But . . . you're . . . It's a serious . . .'

'Shush! The bullet came out, that's the main thing. Help me wrap it up tight . . .'

He'd put the basin on the floor and cut the sheet in two.

'The Baltic gang . . .' he explained. 'They missed me . . . but they didn't miss my poor Torrence . . .'

'Have you disinfected the wound?'

'Yes, I washed it with soap then put some tincture of iodine on it . . .'

'Do you think . . .'

'That's enough for now! . . . With a needle, chief! . . . They anaesthetized him, then killed him with a needle . . .'

Maigret wasn't himself. It was as if he was on the other side of a net curtain that made him look and sound all fuzzy.

'Hand me my shirt . . .'

His voice was blank. His gestures were measured and imprecise. His face was without expression.

'You had to come here . . . Seeing as it's one of our own . . . Not to mention that I didn't want to make waves . . . You can have him taken away later . . . Keep all mention of it out of the papers . . . Chief, you do trust me, don't you?'

All the same there was a catch in Maigret's voice. It touched the super, who took him by the hand.

'Now tell me, Maigret . . . What's wrong?'

'Nothing . . . I'm quite calm, I swear . . . I don't think I've ever been so calm . . . But now, it's between them and me . . . Do you understand? . . .'

The superintendent helped him get his waistcoat and his jacket on. The dressing changed Maigret's appearance, broadening his waist and making his figure less neat, as if he had rolls of fat.

He looked at himself in the mirror and screwed up his face ironically. He was well aware that he now looked all soft. He'd lost that rock-solid, hard-cased look of a human mountain that he liked his enemies to see.

His face was pale, puffy and streaked with red. He was beginning to get bags under his eyes.

'Thank you, chief. Do you think you can do the necessary, as far as Torrence is concerned?'

'Yes, we can keep it out of the news . . . I'll alert the magistrates . . . I'll go to see the prosecutor in person.'

'Good! I'll get on with the job . . .'

He was tidying his mussed hair as he spoke. Then he walked over to the corpse, stopped in his tracks and asked his colleague:

'I'm allowed to close his eyes, aren't I? . . . I think he would have liked me to do it . . .'

His fingers were shaking. He kept them on the dead man's eyelids for a while, as if he was stroking them. The superintendent became agitated and begged him:

'Maigret! Please . . .'

The inspector got up and cast a last glance around the room.

'Farewell, chief . . . Don't let them tell my wife I've been hurt . . .'

His vast bulk filled the whole doorway for a moment.

The Superintendent of Criminal Investigation almost called him back in, because he was a worrying sight.

During the war comrades in arms had said farewell to him just like that, calmly, with the same unreal gentleness, before going over the top.

Those men had never come back!

9. The Hit-man

International gangsters who engage in top-flight scams rarely commit murder. You can take it as a general rule that they never kill – at least, not the people they've chosen to unburden of a million or two. They use more scientific methods of thievery. Most of those gentlemen don't carry guns.

But they do sometimes use elimination to settle scores. Every year, one or two crimes that will never be properly solved take place somewhere. Most often, the victim is unidentifiable, and is buried under a patently false name.

The dead are either snitches, or men who drank too much and blabbed under the influence, or underlings aiming to rise, thus threatening the sitting hierarchy.

In America, the home of specialization, these kinds of execution are never carried out by a gang member. Specialists called hit-men are used. Like official executioners, they have their own teams and rates of remuneration.

The same has sometimes occurred in Europe, notably in the famous case of the Polish Connection (whose leaders all ended up on the scaffold). That set-up carried out several murders on behalf of more highly placed crooks who were keen not to have blood on their own hands.

Maigret knew all that as he went down the stairs towards the front desk of the Majestic.

'When a customer calls down for room service, where does his call get directed?' he asked.

'He gets connected to the room service manager.'

'At night, as well?'

'Sorry! After nine in the evening, night staff deal with it.'

'And where can I find the night staff?'

'In the basement.'

'Take me there.'

Maigret ventured once more into the innards of this hive of luxury designed to cater for a thousand guests. He found an employee sitting at a telephone exchange in a cubby-hole next to the kitchen. He had a register at his desk. It was the quiet time.

'Did Inspector Torrence call down between 9 p.m. and 2 a.m.?'

'Torrence?'

'The officer in the blue room, next door to suite 3 . . .' the receptionist explained in the language of the house.

The reasoning was elementary. Torrence had been attacked in the room by someone who had necessarily entered it. The murderer must have got behind his victim in order to put the chloroform gag over his face. And Torrence hadn't suspected a thing.

Only a hotel valet could have got away with it. He had either been called up by the policeman or else he'd come in unprompted, to clear the table.

Keeping quite calm, Maigret put the question another way round:

'Which member of staff knocked off early last night?'

The operator was taken aback by the question.

'How did you know? Sheer coincidence . . . Pepito got a call telling him his brother was sick . . .'

'What time?'

'Around ten . . .'

'Where was he, at that point?'

'Upstairs.'

'On which telephone did he take the call?'

They called the main exchange. The operator confirmed that he'd not put any call through to Pepito.

Things were moving fast! But Maigret remained placid and glum.

'His card? . . . You must have an employee card . . .'

'Not a proper one . . . We don't keep files on what we call room staff; there's too much turnover.'

They had to go to the hotel office, which was unmanned at that hour. Nonetheless Maigret had them open up the employee records, where he found what he was looking for:

Pepito Moretto, Hôtel Beauséjour, 3, Rue des Batignolles. Appointed on . . .

'Get me Hôtel Beauséjour on the telephone . . .'

Meanwhile Maigret interrogated another employee and learned that Pepito Moretto had been recommended by an Italian maître d'hôtel and had joined the staff of the Majestic three days before the Mortimer-Levingstons' arrival. No complaints about his work. He'd begun in the dining room, but then transferred to room service at his own request.

Hôtel Beauséjour came on the line.

'Hello! . . . Can you get Pepito Moretto to come to the phone? . . . Hello! . . . What was that? . . . His luggage too? . . . Three a.m.? . . . Thank you! . . . Hello? . . . One more thing . . . Did he get any mail at the hotel? . . . No letters at all? . . . Thank you! . . . That's all.'

Maigret hung up, remaining as unnaturally calm as he ever was.

'What's the time?' he asked.

'Five ten . . .'

'Call me a cab.'

He gave the driver the address of Pickwick's Bar.

'You know it closes at 4 a.m.?'

'Doesn't matter.'

The car came to a stop outside the nightclub. It was shuttered, but a streak of light could be seen coming from under the door. Maigret was aware that in most late-night venues the staff – often forty strong – usually has a meal before going home.

They eat in the same room that the customers have just vacated even while the streamers are being tidied away and the cleaners get to work.

Despite that, he didn't ring the bell at Pickwick's. He turned his back on the club, and his eye alighted on a café-tobacconist's at the corner of Rue Fontaine, the sort of place where nightclub staff often gather during intervals or after work.

The bar was still open. When Maigret walked in there were three men with their elbows on the counter, sipping coffee with something stronger in it, talking business.

'Is Pepito not in tonight?'

'He left quite a while ago,' the barman replied.

Maigret noticed that one of the customers who had perhaps recognized him was gesturing at the barman to keep his mouth shut.

'We had an appointment at two . . .' he said.

'He was here . . .'

'I know! . . . I told the dancer from over the road to bring a message to him.'

'You mean José . . . ?'

'Correct. He was supposed to tell Pepito I couldn't make it.'

'José did come over, actually . . . I think they had a chat . . .'

The customer who'd gestured to the barman was now drumming his fingers on the counter. He was pale with fury, because the few sentences that had just been said in the café were all that was needed to explain what had happened.

Around ten or a little before, Pepito had murdered Torrence at the Majestic. He must have had detailed instructions, because he knocked off work straight away, on the excuse that he'd had a phone call from his brother, and came straight to the bar at the corner of Rue Fontaine. Then he waited.

At some point the dancer who'd just been named as José came over the road and passed Pepito a message that a child could guess: shoot Maigret as soon as he steps outside Pickwick's Bar.

In other words, with two crimes in a few hours, the only two people who posed a threat to the Baltic gang would be got rid of!

Pepito fired his gun and fled. His role was over. He hadn't been seen. So he could go and get his bags from Hôtel Beauséjour . . .

Maigret paid for his drink, went out, looked back over his shoulder and saw the three customers vigorously upbraiding the barman.

He knocked at the door of Pickwick's Bar, and a cleaner opened it for him.

As he'd thought, the employees were having a late supper

at tables that had been put end-to-end to make a refectory. Chicken leftovers, pieces of partridge, hors d'œuvres – everything that the customers hadn't eaten. Thirty pairs of eyes turned towards the inspector.

'Has José been gone long?'

'Sure! . . . Straight after . . .'

But the head waiter, recognizing Maigret, whom he'd served, stuck his elbow in the ribs of the man who was talking.

Maigret wasn't fooled.

'Give me his address! And it had better be the right one, OK? Or else you'll be sorry . . .'

'I don't have it . . . Only the boss has . . .'

'Where is he?'

'On his estate, at La Varenne.'

'Give me the books.'

'But . . .'

'Shut up!'

They pretended to look in the drawers of a small office desk behind the podium. Maigret shoved his way into the group that was fiddling about and found the staff register straight away.

José Latourie, 71, Rue Lepic

He exited in the same ponderous manner as he'd come in, while the still-worried waiters went back to their meal.

It was no distance to Rue Lepic. But no. 71 is a long way up the hillside street, and Maigret had to stop twice to get his puff back.

At last he got to the door of a lodging house of the same general kind as Hôtel Beauséjour, though more sordid still. He rang, and the front door opened automatically.

He knocked at a glass window, and the night porter eventually got out of bed for him.

'José Latourie?'

'Still out. His key's here . . .'

'Hand it over! Police! . . .'

'But . . .'

'At the double! . . .'

The fact is, nobody could stand in Maigret's way that night. Yet he wasn't his usual stern and rigid self. Maybe people could sense something even worse?

'Which floor?'

'Fourth!'

The long and narrow room had a stuffy smell. The bed hadn't been made. Like most other people in the same line of trade, José must have slept until four in the afternoon, and hotels don't make up beds later than that.

An old pair of pyjamas that had worn through at the collar and elbows was flung across the sheets. On the floor lay a pair of moccasins with worn soles and broken uppers that must have been used as bedroom slippers. There was a travelling bag in imitation leather, but all it had in it were old newspapers and a patched-up pair of black trousers.

Over the sink was a bar of soap, a pot of skin cream, aspirin tablets and a tube of barbitone. Maigret picked up a ball of scrap paper from the floor and smoothed it out with care. He only needed one sniff to know that it had contained heroin.

Fifteen minutes later Inspector Maigret had gone through the room from top to bottom, but then he noticed a slit in the upholstery of the only armchair in the room. He slipped his finger inside the stuffing and pulled out, one by one, eleven one-gram packs of the same drug.

He put them in his wallet and went back down the stairs. He hailed a city policeman at Place Blanche and gave him instructions. The copper went to stand sentry next to no. 71.

Maigret thought back on the black-haired young man: an uneasy gigolo with unsteady eyes who'd bumped into his table out of agitation when he'd come back from his appointment with Moretto.

Once he'd done the job he hadn't dared go back home, as he would rather lose the few rags that he had and those eleven sachets, which must have had a street price of at least 1,000 francs. He'd be nabbed sooner or later, because he didn't have the nerve. He must have been scared stiff.

Pepito was a cooler kind of customer. Maybe he was in a railway station waiting for the first train out. Maybe he'd gone to ground in the suburbs. Or maybe he'd just moved to a different doss-house in another part of Paris.

Maigret hailed a cab and was on the point of asking for the Majestic when he reckoned they wouldn't have finished the job yet. That's to say, Torrence would still be there.

'Quai des Orfèvres . . .'

As he walked past Jean, Maigret realized that the doorman already knew, and he averted his eyes like a guilty man.

He didn't tend to his stove. He didn't take off his jacket or collar.

He sat at his desk, leaning on his elbows, stock still, for two hours. It was already light when he took notice of a screed that must have been put on his pad at some point during the night.

For the eyes of Detective Chief Inspector Maigret. Urgent.

Around 23.30 man in tails entered Hôtel du Roi de Sicile. Stayed ten minutes. Left in a limousine. The Russian did not exit.

Maigret took it in his stride. And then more news started flooding in. First there was a call from the Courcelles police station, in the seventeenth arrondissement:

'A man by the name of José Latourie, a professional dancer, has been found dead by the railings of Parc Monceau. Three knife wounds. His wallet was not taken. The time and circumstances of the crime have not been established.'

But Maigret knew what they were! He could see Pepito Moretto tailing the young man when he came out of Pickwick's and then, reckoning he was too upset and therefore likely to give the game away, Moretto took his life without even bothering to remove the man's wallet or ID – as a taunt, perhaps. As if to say, 'You think you can use this guy as a lead to get back to us? Be my guest! You can have him!'

Eight thirty. The manager of the Majestic was on the line:

'Hello? . . . Inspector Maigret? . . . It's unbelievable, incredible . . . A few minutes ago no. 17 rang! . . . No. 17! . . . Do you remember? . . . The man who . . .'

'Yes, he's called Oswald Oppenheim . . . Well?'

'I sent up a valet . . . Oppenheim was in bed, cool as a cucumber. He wanted his breakfast.'

10. *The Return of Oswald Oppenheim*

Maigret hadn't moved a muscle for two hours. When he wanted to get up he could barely lift his arm and he had to ring Jean to come and help him put on his overcoat.

'Get me a cab . . .'

A few minutes later he was in the surgery of Dr Lecourbe in Rue Monsieur-le-Prince. There were six people in the waiting room, but he was taken through the living quarters and, as soon as the doctor was free, he was shown into the consulting room.

It took an hour. His body was stiffer. The bags under his eyes were so deep that Maigret looked different, as if he'd got make-up on.

'Rue du Roi-de-Sicile! I'll tell you where to stop . . .'

From far off he caught sight of his two officers walking up and down opposite the lodging house. He got out of the car and went over to them.

'Still inside?'

'Yes . . . There's been one of us on duty at all times . . .'

'Who left the building?'

'A little old man all bent double, then two youngsters, then a woman of about thirty . . .'

'Did the old man have a beard?'

'Yes . . .'

He went off without saying another word, climbed the

narrow staircase and went past the concierge's office. A moment later he was shaking the door of room 32. A woman's voice responded in a language he couldn't identify. The door gave way, and he set eyes on a half-naked Anna Gorskin getting out of bed.

'Where's your boyfriend?' he asked.

He spoke in staccato, like a man in a hurry, and didn't bother to look over the premises.

Anna Gorskin shouted:

'Get out of here! . . . You've no right . . .'

But he stayed unmoved, and picked up off the floor a trenchcoat he knew well. He seemed to be looking for something else. He noticed Fyodor Yurevich's dirty grey trousers at the foot of the bed.

On the other hand there were no men's socks to be found in the room.

The Jewish woman glowered ferociously at the inspector as she put on her dressing gown.

'You think that just because we're foreign . . .'

Maigret didn't give her time to throw a tantrum. He went out quietly and closed the door, which she opened again before he had gone down one flight. She stood on the landing just breathing heavily, not saying a word. She leaned over the railing, staring at him, and then, unable to contain her imperious need to do *something*, she spat on him.

Her spittle fell with a dull thud a metre away.

Inspector Dufour asked:

'Well? . . .'

'Keep a watch on the woman . . . At any rate, she can't disguise herself as an old man.'

'You mean that . . .'

No! He didn't mean anything! He wasn't up to having an argument. He got back in the taxi.

'To the Majestic . . .'

The junior detective was downcast as he watched Maigret leave.

'Do your best!' Maigret called out to him. He didn't want to take it out on the young man. It wasn't his fault if he'd been taken for a ride. After all, hadn't Maigret himself let Torrence get killed?

The manager was waiting for him at the door, which was a new departure for him.

'At last! . . . You see . . . I don't know what do to do any more . . . They came to fetch your . . . your friend . . . They reassured me it would not be in the papers . . . But the *other one* is here! He's here! . . .'

'Nobody saw him come in?'

'Nobody! . . . That's what . . . Listen! . . . Like I told you on the telephone, he rang . . . When the valet went in, he ordered a coffee . . . He was in bed . . .'

'What about Mortimer? . . .'

'Do you think they're connected? . . . That's impossible! He's a well-known figure . . . He's had ministers and bankers call on him right here . . .'

'What's Oppenheim up to now? . . .'

'He's just had a bath . . . I think he's getting dressed . . .'

'And Mortimer?'

'The Mortimers haven't rung yet . . . They're still asleep . . .'

'Give me a description of Pepito Moretto . . .'

'Certainly . . . What I've heard . . . Actually, I never set eyes on him myself . . . I mean, noticed him . . . We have so many employees! . . . But I did some research . . . Short, dark skin, black hair, broad shoulders, could go for days without saying a word . . .'

Maigret copied it all down on a scrap of paper that he put in an envelope that he then addressed to the super. That ought to be enough, combined with the fingerprints that must have been found in the room where Torrence died.

'Have this taken to Quai des Orfèvres . . .'

'Certainly, sir . . .'

The manager was more pliant now because he sensed that events could easily get out of hand, to disastrous effect.

'What are you going to do, inspector?'

But Maigret had already moved off and was standing all clumsy and awkward in the middle of the lobby. He looked like a tourist in a historic church trying to work out without the help of a guide what there was to inspect.

There was a ray of sunshine shedding golden light on the entire lobby of the Majestic. At nine in the morning it was almost deserted. Just a few travellers at separate tables having breakfast while reading the papers.

In the end Maigret slumped into a wicker chair next to the fountain, which for one reason or another wasn't working that morning. The goldfish in the ceramic pond had decided to stop swimming about, and the only thing moving were fish-jaws going up and down, chewing water.

They reminded the inspector of Torrence's open mouth. That must have made a strong impression on him, because he wriggled about for a long time before finding a comfortable position.

A sprinkling of flunkeys passed by from time to time.

Maigret did not take his eyes off them, because he knew that a bullet could fly at any moment.

The game he was in had got near to show-down.

The fact that Maigret had unmasked the identity of Oppenheim, alias Pietr the Latvian, was no big deal. In itself it didn't put the detective at risk.

The Latvian was hardly in hiding. On the contrary, he was flaunting himself in front of his trackers, as he was confident they had nothing on him.

The proof of that was the flurry of telegrams that had tracked him step by step from Krakow to Bremen, from Bremen to Amsterdam, and from Amsterdam to Brussels and Paris.

But then came the corpse on the Étoile du Nord! Most of all, there was Maigret's discovery of the unexpected relations between the East European and Mortimer-Levingston.

And that was a major discovery!

Pietr was a self-avowed crook who was happy to taunt international police forces: 'Just try to catch me red-handed!'

Mortimer was, in the eyes of the whole world, an honest and upright man!

There were just two people who might have guessed the connection between them.

That very evening, Torrence was murdered! And Maigret came under fire from a revolver in Rue Fontaine!

A third, bewildered person, who probably knew next to nothing but might serve as a lead to further investigation, had also been eliminated: José Latourie, a professional dancer.

So Mortimer and the Latvian, presumably reassured

by the three disposals, had gone back to their allotted places. There they were upstairs, in their luxury suites, giving orders on the telephone to a whole team of domestics of a five-star hotel, taking baths, eating meals, getting dressed.

Maigret was waiting for them on his own. He wasn't comfortable in his wicker chair: one side of his chest was stiff and throbbing, and he could barely use his right arm, because it was wracked by persistent pain.

He could have arrested them there and then. But he knew that wouldn't be any use. At most he might get someone to testify against Pietr the Latvian, alias Fyodor Yurevich, alias Oswald Oppenheim, and who must have had many other identities as well, including that of Olaf Swaan.

But what had he got against the American millionaire Mortimer-Levingston? Within an hour of arrest, the US Embassy would lodge a protest! The French banks and companies and financial institutions on whose boards he sat would wheel in political support.

What evidence did he have? What clues? The fact that he'd vanished for a few hours when Pietr was also absent?

That he'd had supper at Pickwick's Bar and that his wife had danced with José Latourie?

That a police sergeant had seen him go into a scruffy lodging house at the sign of the Roi de Sicile?

It would all be torn to shreds! Apologies would have to be made and, to satisfy the Americans, there would have to be a scapegoat. Maigret would be sacked, at least for show.

But Torrence was dead!

He must have been carried across the hall at the crack of dawn on a stretcher. Or else the manager had warded off the possibility of an early riser seeing such an unpleasant spectacle by having the corpse taken out by the service entrance!

That was very likely! Narrow corridors, spiral staircases . . . the stretcher would have bumped into the railings . . .

Behind the mahogany counter the telephones rang. Comings and goings. Hurried commands. The manager came up to him:

'Mrs Mortimer-Levingston is leaving . . . They've just rung from upstairs to have her trunk brought down . . . The car is waiting . . .'

Maigret smiled faintly.

'Which train?'

'She's flying to Berlin from Le Bourget airfield . . .'

He'd barely finished his sentence when she appeared, dressed in a light-grey travelling cape, carrying a crocodile-skin handbag. She was moving quickly but when she got to the revolving door she couldn't resist turning round.

Maigret made a great effort to stand up so as to be certain she would see him. He was sure she had bitten her lip. Then she left even more hurriedly, waving her hands about and giving orders to her chauffeur.

The manager was wanted elsewhere. The inspector was all on his own beside the fountain, which suddenly began to spout. It must have been on a time-clock.

It was 10 a.m.

Maigret smiled inwardly, sat down weightily but with great care, because the slightest movement pulled on his wound, which was hurting him more and more.

'You get rid of the weakest links . . .'

That's what it was! First José Latourie, reckoned to be unreliable, had been got rid of with three stabs; and now Mrs Mortimer, who was also quite emotional.

They were packing her off to Berlin! And doing her a favour.

The tough guys were staying behind: Pietr, who was taking ages to get dressed; Mortimer-Levingston, who had probably not lost an ounce of his aristocratic grandeur; and Pepito Moretto, the team's hit-man.

Connected by invisible threads, all three were gearing themselves up.

The enemy was in their midst, in a wicker armchair, sitting quite still with his legs stretched out in the middle of the lobby as the hotel began to get busier. Haze from the tinkling fountain misted his face.

The lift came down and stopped.

The first to emerge was Pietr, wearing a beautifully tailored cinnamon-coloured suit and smoking a Henry Clay cigar.

He was master of the house. That was what he paid for. Casually, confidently, he sauntered round the hall, stopped here and there, looked into the showcases that prestige shops set up in the lobbies of grand hotels, glanced at the board displaying the latest foreign currency rates and finally took up position less than three metres away from Maigret to stare at the artificial-looking goldfish in the pond. He flicked cigar ash into the water and then sailed off to the library.

11. *Arrivals and Departures*

Pietr glanced through a few newspapers, paying particular attention to the *Revaler Bote*, from Tallinn. There was only one out-of-date issue at the Majestic. It had probably been left behind by another guest.

He lit another cigar at a few minutes to eleven, went across the lobby and sent a bellhop to fetch his hat.

Thanks to the sun falling on one side of the Champs-Élysées, it was quite mild.

Pietr went out without his coat, with just a grey homburg on his head, and walked slowly up to the Arc de Triomphe like a man out for a breath of fresh air.

Maigret kept fairly close behind, making no effort to remain unseen. As the dressing on his wound made moving about uncomfortable, he did not appreciate the walk.

At the corner of Rue de Berry he heard a whistle that wasn't very loud and took no notice of it. Then another whistle. So he turned round and saw Inspector Dufour performing a mystifying dumb show so as to let him know he had something to tell him.

Dufour was in Rue de Berry, pretending to be fascinated by a pharmacist's window display, so his gesticulations appeared to be addressed to a waxwork female head, one of whose cheeks was covered with a meticulous simulation of eczema.

'Come over here . . . Come on! Quickly . . .'

Dufour was offended and indignant. He'd been prowling around the Majestic for an hour, using every trick of the trade – and now his chief was ordering him to break cover all at once!

'What's happened?'

'The Jewish woman . . .'

'She went out?'

'She's here . . . And since you made me cross over, she can see us, right now . . .'

Maigret looked around.

'Where from?'

'From Le Select . . . She's sitting inside . . . Look! The curtain's moving . . .'

'Carry on watching her . . .'

'Openly?'

'Have a drink at the table next to hers, if you like.'

At this point in the game there was no point playing hide-and-seek. Maigret walked on and caught up with Pietr in a couple of hundred metres. He hadn't tried to take advantage of Maigret's conversation with Dufour to slip away.

And why should he slip away? The match was being played on a new pitch. The two sides could see each other. Pretty much all the cards were on the table now.

Pietr walked up and down the Champs-Élysées twice over, from Étoile to the Rond-Point and back again, and by then Maigret had grasped his character, entirely.

He had a slender, tense figure that was fundamentally more thoroughbred than Mortimer's, but his breeding was of a kind particular to Northern peoples.

Maigret was already familiar with the type. He'd met

others of the same ilk in the Latin Quarter during his days as a medical student (though he never completed the course), and they had baffled the Southerner that he was.

He had a particular recollection of one such, a skinny, blond Pole whose hair was already thinning at the age of twenty-two. He was the son of a cleaning lady, and for seven years he came to lectures at the Sorbonne without any socks, living on one egg with a slice of bread a day. He couldn't afford to buy the print versions of the lectures so he had to study in public libraries. He got to know nothing of Paris, of women, or of French ways. But scarcely had he got his degree than he was appointed a senior professor in Warsaw. Five years later Maigret saw him on a return visit to Paris, as a member of a delegation of foreign scientists. He was as skinny and icy as ever, but he went to a dinner at the presidential palace.

Maigret had met others, too. Not all of them were quite so special. But they were all amazingly keen to learn a huge range of different things. And learn they did!

To learn for the sake of learning! Like that Belgian professor who knew all the languages of the Far East – more than forty of them – without ever having set foot in Asia or being at all interested in the peoples whose languages he dissected, to amuse himself.

Ferocious will-power of the same kind could be seen in the grey-green eyes of Pietr the Latvian. But as soon as you thought you could pigeon-hole him in the category of intellectuals, you noticed other features that didn't fit at all.

In a sense you could feel the shadow of Fyodor Yurevich, the Russian vagrant in the trenchcoat, hovering over the neat figure of the guest at the Majestic.

It was a moral certainty that they were one and the same man; their identity was about to become a patent fact as well.

The evening he got to Paris, Pietr went missing. Next morning Maigret caught up with him in Fécamp in the shape of Fyodor Yurevich.

Fyodor returned to Rue du Roi-de-Sicile. A few hours later, Mortimer dropped in on him at his lodging. Several people then came out of the building, including a bearded old man.

Next morning Pietr was back in his place at Hôtel Majestic.

What was astounding was that, apart from a fairly striking physical resemblance, these two incarnations had absolutely nothing in common.

Fyodor Yurevich was a genuine Slavic vagrant, a sentimental and manic *déclassé*. Everything fitted perfectly. He didn't make the slightest error even when he leaned on the counter in the drinking hole in Fécamp.

On the other hand there wasn't a thread out of place in the character of the East European intellectual, breathing refinement from head to toe. The way he asked the bellhop for a light, the way he wore his top-quality English homburg, his casual stroll in the sun along the Champs-Élysées and the way he looked at window-displays – it was all quite perfect.

It was so perfect it had to go deeper than play-acting. Maigret had acted parts himself. Although the police use disguise and deep cover less often than people imagine, they still have to do it from time to time. But Maigret in make-up was still Maigret in some aspect of his being – in a glance, or a tic. When he'd dressed up as a cattle-dealer, for example (he had done that once, and got away with it), he was *acting the role* of a cattle-dealer. But he hadn't *become* a cattle-dealer. The persona he'd put on remained external to him.

Pietr-Fyodor was both Pietr and Fyodor *from inside*.

The inspector's view could be summed up this way: he was both one thing and the other not only in dress but in essence.

He'd been living two quite different lives in alternation for many years, that was clear, and maybe all his life long.

These were just the random thoughts that struck Maigret as he walked slowly through the sweet-smelling light air.

All of a sudden, though, the character of Pietr the Latvian cracked wide open.

What brought this about was significant in itself. He had paused opposite Fouquet's and was about to cross the street, manifestly intending to have an aperitif at the bar of that high-class establishment.

But then he changed his mind. He carried on along the same side of the avenue, then suddenly began to hurry before darting down Rue Washington.

There was café nearby of the sort you find nestled in all the really plush areas of the city, to cater for taxi-drivers and domestic staff.

Pietr went in, and Maigret followed him, opening the door just as the Latvian was ordering an ersatz absinthe.

He was standing at the horseshoe counter. From time to time a waiter in a blue apron gave it a desultory wipe with a dirty dishcloth. There was a knot of dust-covered building workers to the Latvian's left, and, on his right, a gas company cashier.

The leader of the Baltic gang clashed with the surroundings in every detail of his impeccably tasteful and stylish attire.

His blond toothbrush moustache and his thin, almost transparent eyebrows caught the light. He stared at Maigret, not straight on, but in the mirror at the back of the bar.

That's when the inspector noticed a quiver in Pietr's lips and an almost imperceptible contraction of his nostrils.

Pietr must have been watching himself in the mirror too. He started drinking slowly, but soon he gulped down what was left in his glass in one go and waved a finger to say:

'Same again!'

Maigret had ordered a vermouth. He looked even taller and wider than ever in the confined space of the bar. He didn't take his eyes off the Latvian.

He was having something like double vision. Just as had happened to him in the hotel lobby, he could see one image superimposed on another: behind the current scene, he had a vision of the squalid bar in Fécamp. Pietr was going double. Maigret could see him in his cinnamon suit and in his worn-out raincoat at the same time.

'I'm telling you I'd rather do that than get beaten up!' one of the builders exclaimed, banging his glass down on the counter.

Pietr was now on his third glass of green liquid. Maigret could smell the aniseed in it. Because the gas company cashier had moved away, he was now shoulder to shoulder with his target, at touching distance.

Maigret was two heads taller than Pietr. They were both facing the mirror, and gazed at each other in that pewter-tinted screen.

The Latvian's face began to decompose, starting with his eyes. He snapped his white dry-skinned fingers, then wiped his forehead with his hand. A struggle then slowly began on his face. In the mirror Maigret saw now the guest of the Majestic, now the face of Anna Gorskin's tormented lover.

But the second visage didn't emerge in full. It kept getting pushed back by immense muscular effort. Only the eyes of Pietr's Russian self stayed stable.

He was hanging on to the edge of the counter with his left hand. His body was swaying.

Maigret tried out an experiment. In his pocket he still had the photograph of Madame Swaan that he'd extracted from the archive album of the photographer in Fécamp.

'How much do I owe you?' he asked the barman.

'Two francs twenty . . .'

He pretended to look for the money in his wallet and managed to drop the snapshot into a puddle of spilt drink between the counter's raised edges. He paid no attention to it, and held out a five franc note. But he looked hard at the mirror.

The waiter picked the photograph up and started wiping it clean, apologetically.

Pietr was squeezing the glass in his hand. His face was rigid and his eyes were hard.

Then suddenly there was an unexpected noise, a soft but sharp crack that made the barman at the cash register turn round with a start.

Pietr opened his fist. Shards of broken glass tinkled on to the counter.

He'd gradually crushed it. He was bleeding from a small cut on his index finger. He threw down a 100 franc note and left the bar without looking at Maigret.

Now he was striding straight towards the Majestic, showing no sign of drunkenness. His gait was just as neat and his posture just the same as when he had left it. Maigret stuck obstinately to his heels. As he got within sight of the hotel he recognized a car pulling away. It belonged to the forensics lab and must have been taking away the cameras and other equipment used for fingerprint detection.

This encounter stopped him in his tracks. His confidence sagged: he felt unmoored, without a post to lean on.

He passed by Le Select. Through the window Inspector Dufour waved his arm in what was supposed to be a confidential gesture but could be understood by anyone with eyes as an invitation to look at the table where the Jewish woman was sitting.

Maigret went up to the front desk at the Majestic:

'Mortimer?'

'He's just been driven to the American Embassy, where he's having lunch . . .'

Pietr was on his way to his seat in the empty dining room.

'Will you be lunching with us, sir?' the manager asked Maigret.

'Lay me a setting opposite that man, thank you.'

The hotelier found that hard to swallow.

'Opposite? . . .' he sputtered. 'I can't do that! The room is empty and . . .'

'I said, opposite.'

The manager would not give up and ran after the detective.

'Listen! It will surely cause a to-do . . . I can put you at a table where you'll be able to see him just as well.'

'I said, at his table.'

It was then, pacing about the lobby, that he realized he was weary. Weary with an insidious lassitude that affected him all over, and his whole self besides, body and soul.

He slumped into the wicker chair he had sat in that morning. A couple consisting of a lady ripe in years and an overdressed young man stood up straight away. From behind her lorgnette the woman said in a voice that was meant to be overheard:

'These five-stars aren't what they used to be . . . Did you see that . . .'

'That' was Maigret. And he didn't even smile back.

12. A Woman With a Gun

'Hello! . . . Err . . . Um . . . Is that you?'

'Maigret speaking,' the inspector sighed. He'd recognized Dufour's voice.

'Shush! . . . I'll keep it short, chief . . . Went toilet . . . Handbag on table . . . Looked . . . Gun inside!'

'Is she still at Le Select?'

'She's eating . . .'

Dufour must have looked like a cartoon conspirator in the telephone booth, waving his arms about in mysterious and terrified ways. Maigret hung up without a word as he didn't have the heart to respond. Little foibles which usually made him smile now made him feel almost physically sick.

The manager had resigned himself to laying a place for Maigret opposite the Latvian, who'd asked the waiter:

'In whose honour . . . ?'

'I can't say, sir. I do as I'm told . . .'

So he let it drop. An English family group of five burst into the dining room and warmed up the atmosphere a bit.

Maigret deposited his overcoat and hat in the cloakroom, walked across the dining room and halted for a moment before sitting down. He even made as if to say hello.

But Pietr didn't seem to notice him. The four or five glasses of spirits he'd drunk seemed to have been forgotten. He conducted himself with icily impeccable manners.

He gave not the slightest hint of nerves. With his gaze

on a far horizon, he looked more like an engineer trying to solve some technical problem in his head.

He drank modestly, though he'd selected one of the best burgundies of the last two decades.

He ate a light meal: omelette *aux fines herbes*, veal cutlet in crème fraîche.

In the intervals between the dishes he sat patiently with his two hands flat on the table, paying no attention to what was going on around him.

The dining room was beginning to fill up.

'Your moustache is coming unstuck', Maigret said suddenly.

Pietr didn't react. After a while he just stroked his lips with two fingers. Maigret was right, though it was hardly noticeable.

Maigret's imperturbability was legendary among his colleagues, but even so he was having trouble holding himself back.

He was going to have an even tougher time of it that afternoon.

Obviously he did not expect Pietr to do anything to put himself in jeopardy, given the close surveillance. All the same, he'd surely taken one step towards disaster in the morning. Wasn't it reasonable to hope he would be pushed all the way down by the unremitting presence of a man acting like a blank wall, shutting him off from the light?

Pietr had coffee in the lobby and then asked for his lightweight overcoat to be brought down. He strolled down the Champs-Élysées and a little after two went into a local cinema.

He didn't come out until six. He'd not spoken to anyone, not written anything, nor made a move that was in any way suspicious.

Sitting comfortably in his seat he'd concentrated on following the twists and turns of an infantile plot.

If he'd looked over his shoulder as he then sauntered towards Place de l'Opéra to have his aperitif he'd have realized that the figure behind him was made of tough, persistent stuff. But he might also have sensed that the inspector was beginning to doubt his own judgement.

That was indeed the case. In the darkness of the cinema, doing his best not to watch the images flickering on the screen, Maigret kept on thinking about what would happen if he were to make an arrest on the spot.

But he knew very well what would happen! No convincing material evidence on his side. On the other side, a heavy web of influence weighing on the examining magistrate, the prosecutor, going right up to the foreign minister and the minister of justice!

He was slightly hunched as he walked. His wound was hurting, and his right arm was getting even stiffer. The doctor had said firmly:

'If the pain starts to get worse, come back here straight away! It'll mean you've got an infection in the wound . . .'

So what? Did he have time to bother about that?

'Did you see that?' a guest at the Majestic had said that morning.

Heavens above, yes! 'That' was a cop trying to stop leading criminals from doing any more harm, a cop set on avenging a colleague who'd been murdered in that very same five-star hotel!

'That' didn't have a tailor in London, he didn't have time to get manicured every morning, and his wife had been cooking meals for him for three days in a row without knowing what was going on.

'That' was a senior detective earning 2,200 francs a month who, when he'd solved a case and put criminals behind bars, had to sit down with paper and pencil and itemize his expenses, clip his receipts and documentation to the claim, and then go and argue it out with accounts!

Maigret had no car of his own, no millions, not even a big team. If he commandeered a city policeman or two, he still had to justify the use he made of them.

Pietr, who was sitting a metre away from him, paid for a drink with a 50 franc note and didn't bother to pick up the change. It was either a habit or a trick. Then, presumably to irritate the inspector, he went into a shirt-maker's and spent half an hour picking twelve ties and three dressing gowns. He left his calling card on the counter while a smartly dressed salesman scurried after him.

The lesion was definitely becoming inflamed. Sometimes he had intense shooting pains in the whole of his shoulder and he felt like vomiting, as if he had a stomach infection as well.

Rue de la Paix, Place Vendôme, Faubourg Saint-Honoré! Pietr was gadding about . . .

Back to the Majestic at last . . . The bellhops rushed to help him with the revolving door.

'Chief . . .'

'You again?'

Officer Dufour emerged tentatively from the shadows with a worried look in his eyes.

'Listen . . . She's vanished . . .'

'What are you talking about?'

'I did my best, I promise! She left Le Select. A minute later she went into a couturier's at no. 52. I waited an hour and then interrogated the doorman. She hadn't been seen in the first-floor showroom. She'd simply walked straight through, because the building has a second exit on Rue de Berry.'

'That's enough!'

'What should I do?'

'Take a break!'

Dufour looked Maigret in the eye, then turned his gaze sharply aside.

'I swear to you that . . .'

To his amazement, Maigret patted him on the shoulder.

'You're a good lad, Dufour! Don't let it get you down . . .'

Then he went inside the Majestic, saw the manager making a face and smiled back.

'Oppenheim?'

'He's just gone up to his room.'

Maigret saw a lift that was free.

'Second floor . . .'

He filled his pipe and suddenly realized with another smile that was somewhat more ironical than the first that for the last several hours he'd forgotten to have a smoke.

He went to the door of no. 17 and didn't waver. He knocked. A voice told him to come in. He did so, closing the door behind him.

Despite the radiators a log fire had been lit in the lounge, for decoration. The Latvian was leaning on the mantelpiece and pushing a piece of paper towards the flames with his toe, to get it to light.

At a glance Maigret saw that he was not as cool as before, but he had enough self-control not to show how much that pleased him.

He picked up a dainty gilded chair with his huge hand, carried it to within a metre of the fire, set it down on its slender legs and sat astride it.

Maybe it was because he had his pipe back between his teeth. Or maybe because his whole being was rebounding from the hours of depression, or rather, of uncertainty, that he'd just been through.

In any case, the fact is he was now tougher and weightier than ever. He was Maigret twice over, so to speak. Carved from a single piece of old oak, or, better still, from very dense stone.

He propped his elbows on the back of the chair. You could feel that if he was driven to an extremity he could grab his target by the scruff of his neck with his two broad hands and bang his head against the wall.

'Mortimer is back,' he said.

The Latvian watched the paper burn, then slowly looked up.

'I'm not aware . . .'

It did not escape Maigret's eye that Pietr's fists were clenched. It also did not escape him that there was a suitcase next to the bedroom door that had not been in the suite before. It was a common suitcase that cost 100 francs at most, and it clashed with the surroundings.

'What's inside that?'

No answer. Just a nervous twitch. Then a question:

'Are you going to arrest me?'

He was anxious, to be sure, but there was also a sense of relief in his voice.

'Not yet . . .'

Maigret got up and pushed the suitcase across the floor with his foot, and then bent down to open it.

It contained a brand-new grey off-the-peg suit, with its tags still on it.

The inspector picked up the telephone.

'Hello! . . . Is Mortimer back? . . . No? . . . No callers for no. 17? Hello! . . . Yes . . . A parcel from a shirt-makers on the Grands Boulevards? . . . No need to bring it up . . .'

He put the phone down and carried on interrogating aggressively:

'Where is Anna Gorskin?'

At last he felt he was making progress!

'Look around . . .'

'You mean she's not in this suite . . . But she was here . . . She brought this suitcase, and a letter . . .'

The Latvian gave a quick stab at the charred paper to make it collapse. Now it was just a pile of ash.

Maigret was fully aware that this was no time for careless words. He was on the right track, but the slightest slip would give his advantage away.

Out of sheer habit he got up and went to the fire so abruptly that Pietr flinched and made as if to put up his arms in self-defence, then blushed with embarrassment. Maigret was only going to stand with his back to the fire! He took short, strong puffs at his pipe.

Silence ensued for such a long time and with so much unspoken that it strained nerves to breaking point.

The Latvian was on a tightrope and still putting on a show of balance. In response to Maigret's pipe he lit a cigar.

Maigret started to pace up and down and nearly broke the telephone table when he leaned on it. The Latvian didn't see that he'd pressed the call button without picking up the receiver. The result was instantaneous. The bell rang. It was reception.

'Hello! . . . You called?'

'Hello! . . . Yes . . . What was that?'

'Hello! . . . This is reception . . .'

Cool as a cucumber, Maigret went on:

'Hello! . . . Yes . . . Mortimer! . . . Thank you! . . . I'll drop in on him soon . . .'

'Hello! Hello! . . .'

He'd scarcely put the earpiece back on its hook when the telephone rang again. The manager was cross:

'What's going on? . . . I don't get it . . .'

'Dammit! . . .' Maigret thundered.

He stared heavily at the Latvian, who had gone even paler and who, for at least a second, wanted to make a dash for the door.

'No big deal,' Maigret told him. 'Mortimer-Levingston's just come in. I'd asked them to let me know . . .'

He could see sweat beading on Pietr's brow.

'We were discussing the suitcase and the letter that came with it . . . Anna Gorskin . . .'

'Anna's not involved . . .'

'Excuse me . . . I thought . . . Isn't the letter from her?'

'Listen . . .'

Pietr was shaking. Quite visibly shaking. And he was in a strangely nervous state. He had twitches all over his face and spasms in his body.

'Listen to me . . .'

'I'm listening,' Maigret finally conceded, still standing with his back to the fire.

He'd slipped his good hand into his gun pocket. It would take him no more than a second to aim. He was smiling, but behind the smile you could sense concentration taken to an utmost extreme.

'Well then? I said I was listening . . .'

But Pietr grabbed a bottle of whisky, muttering through clenched teeth:

'What the hell . . .'

Then he poured himself a tumbler and drank it straight off, looking at Maigret with the eyes of Fyodor Yurevich and a dribble of drink glinting on his chin.

13. *The Two Pietrs*

Maigret had never seen a man get drunk at such lightning speed. It's true he had also never seen anyone fill a tumbler to the brim with whisky, knock it back, refill it, knock the second glass back, then do the same a third time before shaking the bottle over his mouth to get the last few drops of 104 degrees proof spirit down his throat.

The effect was impressive. Pietr went crimson and the next minute he was as white as a sheet, with blotches of red on his cheeks. His lips lost their colour. He steadied himself on the low table, staggered about, then said with the detachment of a true drunk:

'This is what you wanted, isn't it? . . .'

He laughed uncertainly, expressing a whole range of things: fear, irony, bitterness and maybe despair. He tried to hold on to a chair but knocked it over, then wiped his damp brow.

'You do realize that you'd never have managed by yourself . . . Sheer luck . . .'

Maigret didn't move. He was so disturbed by the scene that he nearly put an end to it by having the man drink or inhale an antidote.

What he was watching was the same transformation he'd seen that morning, but on a scale ten times, a hundred times greater.

A few minutes earlier he'd been dealing with a man in

control of himself, with a sharp mind backed up by uncommon willpower . . . A society man, a man of learning, of the utmost elegance.

Now there was just this bag of nerves tugged this way and that as if by a crazy puppeteer, with eyes like tempests set in a wan and twisted face.

And he was laughing! But despite his laughter and his pointless excitement, he had his ear open and was bending over as if he expected to hear something coming up from underneath.

Underneath was the Mortimers' suite.

'We had a first-rate set-up!' His voice was now hoarse. 'You'd never have got to the bottom of it. It was sheer chance, I'm telling you, or rather, several coincidences in a row!'

He bumped into the wall and leaned on it at an oblique angle, screwing up his face because his artificial intoxication – alcohol poisoning, to be more precise – must have given him a dreadful headache.

'Come on, then . . . While there's still time, try and work out which Pietr I am! Quite an actor, aren't I?'

He was sad and disgusting, comical and repulsive at the same time. His level of intoxication was increasing by the second.

'It's odd they're not here yet! But they will be! . . . And then . . . Come on, guess! . . . which Pietr will I be? . . .'

His mood changed abruptly and he put his head in his hands. You could see on his face that he was in pain.

'You'll never understand . . . The story of the two Pietrs . . . It's like the story of Cain and Abel . . . I suppose you're a Catholic . . . In our country we're Protestant and know

the Bible by heart . . . But it's no good . . . I'm sure Cain
was a good-natured boy, a trusting guy . . . Whereas that
Abel . . .'

There was someone in the corridor. The door opened.

It even took Maigret aback, and he had to clench his
pipe harder between his teeth.

For the person who had just come in was Mortimer, in
a fur coat, looking as hale and ruddy as a man who has
just come from a gourmet dinner.

He gave off a faint smell of liqueur and cigar.

His expression altered as soon as he got into the lounge.
Colour drained from his face. Maigret noticed he was
asymmetrical in a way that was difficult to place but which
gave him a murky look.

You could sense he'd just come in from outside. There
was still some cooler air in the folds of his clothes.

There were two sides to the scene. Maigret couldn't
watch both simultaneously.

He paid more attention to the Latvian as he tried to
clear his mind once his initial fright had passed. But it was
already too late. The man had taken too large a dose. He
knew it himself, even as he desperately applied all his will-
power to the task.

His face was twisted. He could probably see people and
things only through a distorting haze. When he let go of
the table he tripped, came within a whisker of falling over
but miraculously recovered his balance.

'My dear Mor . . .' he began.

His eyes crossed Maigret's and he spoke in a different
voice:

'Too bad, eh! Too . . .'

The door slammed. Rapid footsteps going away. Mortimer had beaten a retreat. At that point Pietr fell into an armchair.

Maigret was at the door in a trice. Before setting off, he stopped to listen.

But the many different noises in the hotel made it impossible to identify the sound of Mortimer's footsteps.

'I'm telling you, this is what you wanted . . .' Pietr stuttered, and then with slurred tongue carried on speaking in a language Maigret didn't know.

The inspector locked the door behind him and went along the corridor until he got to a staircase. He ran down.

He got to the first-floor landing just in time to bump into a woman who was running away. He smelt gunpowder.

He grabbed the woman by her clothes with his left hand. With his right hand he hit her wrist hard, and a revolver fell to the floor. The gun went off, and the bullet shattered the glass pane in the lift.

The woman struggled. She was exceptionally strong. Maigret had no means to restrain her other than twisting her wrist, and she fell to her knees, hissing:

'Let go! . . .'

The hotel began to stir. An unaccustomed sound of excitement arose along all the corridors and filtered out all the exits.

The first person to appear was a chambermaid dressed in black and white. She raised her arms and fled in fright.

'Don't move!' Maigret ordered – not to the maid, but to his prisoner.

But both women froze. The chambermaid screamed:

'Mercy! . . . I haven't done anything . . .'

Then things turned quite chaotic. People started pouring in from every direction. The manager was waving his arms about in the middle of the crowd. Further down there were women in evening dress making a terrible din.

Maigret decided to bend over and put handcuffs on his prisoner, who was none other than Anna Gorskin. She fought back, and in the struggle her dress got torn, making her bosom visible, as it often was. A fine figure of a woman she was too, with her sparkling eyes and her twisted mouth.

'Mortimer's suite . . .' Maigret shouted to the manager.

But the poor man didn't know if he was coming or going. Maigret was on his own in the middle of a panicky crowd of people who kept bumping into each other, with womenfolk screaming, weeping and falling over.

The American's suite was only a few metres away. The inspector didn't need to open the door, it was swinging on its hinges. He saw a body on the floor, bleeding but still moving. Then he ran back up to the next floor, banged on the door he'd locked himself, got no response, and then forced it open.

Pietr's suite was empty!

The suitcase was still on the floor where he had left it, with the off-the-peg suit laid over it.

An icy blast came from the open window. It gave on to a courtyard no wider than a chimney. Down below you could make out the dark rectangular shapes of three doors.

Maigret went back down with heavy tread. The crowd had calmed down somewhat. One of the guests was a doctor. But the women – like the men, moreover! – weren't too bothered about Mortimer, to whom the doctor was attending. All eyes were on the Jewish woman slumped in the corridor with handcuffs on her wrists, snarling insults and threats at her audience. Her hat had slipped off and bunches of glossy hair fell over her face.

A desk interpreter came out of the lift with the broken glass, accompanied by a city policeman.

'Get them all out of here,' Maigret ordered. People protested behind his back. He looked big enough to fill the whole width of the corridor. Grumpily, obstinately, he went over to Mortimer's body.

'Well? . . .'

The doctor was a German with not much French, and he launched into a long explanation in a medley of two languages.

The millionaire's lower jaw had literally vanished. There was just a wide, red-black mess in its place. Despite this, his mouth was still moving, though it wasn't quite a mouth any more, and from it came a babbling sound, with a lot of blood.

Nobody could understand what it meant, neither Maigret nor the doctor who was, it turned out later, a professor at the University of Bonn; nor could the two or three other persons standing nearest.

Cigar ash was sprinkled over the fur coat. One of Mortimer's hands was wide open.

'Is he dead?' Maigret asked.

The doctor shook his head, and both men fell silent.

The noise in the corridor was abating. The policeman was moving the insistent rubberneckers down the corridor one pace at a time.

Mortimer's lips closed and then opened again. The

doctor kept still for a few seconds. Then he rose and, as if relieved of a great weight, declared:

'Dead, *ja* . . . It was hard . . .'

Someone had stepped on the fur coat, which bore a clear imprint of the sole of a shoe.

The policeman, with his silver epaulettes, appeared in the open doorway and didn't say anything at first.

'What should I . . .'

'Get them all out of here, every single one . . .' Maigret commanded.

'The woman is screaming . . .'

'Let her scream . . .'

He went to stand in front of the fireplace. But there was no fire in this hearth.

14. The Ugala Club

Every race has its own smell, and other races hate it. Despite opening the window and puffing relentlessly at his pipe, Inspector Maigret could not get rid of the background odour that made him uncomfortable.

Maybe the whole of Hôtel du Roi de Sicile was impregnated with the smell. Perhaps it was the entire street. The first whiff hits you when the hotel-keeper with the skullcap opens his window, and the further you go up the stairs, the stronger it gets.

In Anna Gorskin's room, it was overpowering. That's partly because there was food all over the place. The *saucisson* was full of garlic but it had gone soft and turned an unprepossessing shade of pink. There were also some fried fish lying on a plate in a vinegary sauce.

Stubs from Russian cigarettes. Half a dozen cups with tea-dregs in them. Sheets and underwear that felt still damp. The tang of a bedroom that has never been aired.

He'd come across a small grey canvas bag inside the mattress that he'd taken apart. A few photos as well as a university diploma dropped out of it.

One of photographs displayed a steep cobbled street of gabled houses of the kind you see in Holland, but painted a bright white to show off the neat black outlines of windows, doors and cornices.

On the house in the foreground was an inscription in

ornate lettering reminiscent of Gothic and Cyrillic script at the same time

6

Rütsep

Max Johannson

Tailor

It was a huge building. There was a beam sticking out from the roof with a pulley on the end used to winch up wheat for storage in the loft. From street level, six steps with an iron railing led up to the main door.

On those steps a family group was gathered round a dull, grey little man of about forty – that must be the tailor – trying to look solemn and superior.

His wife, in a satin dress so tight it might burst, was sitting on a carved chair. She was smiling cheerfully at the photographer, though she'd pursed her lips to make herself look a little more distinguished.

The parents were placed behind two children holding hands. They were both boys, aged around six or eight, in short trousers, black long socks, in white embroidered sailor collar shirts with decorations on the cuffs.

Same age! Same height! A striking likeness between them, and with the tailor.

But you couldn't fail to notice the difference in their characters. One had a decisive expression on his face and was looking at the camera aggressively, with some kind of a challenge. The other was stealing a glance at his brother. It was a look of trust and admiration.

The photographer's name was embossed on the image: *K. Akel, Pskov.*

The second black-and-white photograph was bigger

and more significant. Three refectory tables could be seen lengthwise, laden with bottles and plates, and, at their head, a display-piece made of six flags, a shield with a design that couldn't be made out, two crossed swords and a hunting horn. The diners were students between seventeen and twenty years of age, wearing caps with narrow silver-edged visors and velvet tops which must have been that acid shade of green which is the Germans' favourite colour, and their northern neighbours' too.

They all had short hair and most of their faces were fine-featured. Some of them were smiling unaffectedly at the camera lens. Others were toasting it with an odd kind of beerstein made of turned wood. Some had shut their eyes against the magnesium flare.

Clearly visible in the middle of the table was a slate with the legend:

Ugala Club
Tartu

Students have clubs of that kind in universities all over the world. One young man, however, was separate from the others. He was standing in front of the display without his cap. His shaved head made his face stand out. Unlike most of the others, in lounge suits, this young man was wearing a dinner jacket – a little awkwardly, as it was still too big for his shoulders. Over his white waistcoat he wore a wide sash, as if he'd been made Knight Commander of something. It was the sash of office of the captain of the club.

Curiously, although most of those present looked at the photographer, the really shy ones had turned instinctively towards their leader. Looking at him with the greatest intensity from his side was his double, who had to twist his neck almost out of joint in order to keep his eyes on his brother.

The student with the sash and the one who was gazing at him were unquestionably the same as the lads in front of the house in Pskov, that's to say the sons of tailor Johannson.

The diploma was written in antique-looking script on parchment, in Latin. The text was larded with archaic formulas that appointed one Hans Johannson, a student of philosophy, as a Fellow of the Ugala Club. It was signed at the bottom by the *Grand Master of the Club, Pietr Johannson.*

In the same canvas bag there was another package tied up with string, also containing photographs as well as letters written in Russian.

The photographs were by a professional in Vilna. One of them portrayed a plump and stern-looking middle-aged Jewish lady bedecked with as many jewels as a Catholic reliquary.

A family resemblance with Anna Gorskin was obvious at first glance. There was a photo of her too, aged around sixteen, in an ermine toque.

The correspondence was on paper printed with the tri-lingual letterhead of

Ephraim Gorskin

Wholesale Furrier

Royal Siberian Furs a Specialty

Branches in Vilna and Warsaw

Maigret was unable to translate the handwritten part. But he did at least notice that one heavily underlined phrase recurred several times over.

He slipped these papers into his pocket and conscientiously went over the room one last time. It had been occupied by the same person for such a long time that it had ceased to be just a hotel room. Every object and every detail down to the stains on the wallpaper and the linen told the full story of Anna Gorskin.

There was hair everywhere: thick, oily strands, like Asian hair.

Hundreds of cigarette butts. Tins of dry biscuits; broken biscuits on the floor. A pot of dried ginger. A big preserving jar containing the remains of a goose confit, with a Polish label. Caviar.

Vodka, whisky, and a small vessel, which Maigret sniffed, holding some left-over opium in compressed sheets.

Half an hour later he was at Quai des Orfèvres, listening to a translation of the letters, and he hung on to sentences such as:

'. . . Your mother's legs are swelling more and more . . .'

'. . . Your mother is asking if you still get swollen ankles when you walk a lot, because she thinks you have the same ailment as she does . . .'

'. . . We seem to be safe now, though the Vilna question hasn't been settled. We're caught between the Lithuanians and the Poles . . . But both sides hate the Jews . . .'

'. . . Could you check up on M. Levasseur, 65, Rue d'Hauteville, who has ordered some skins but has not provided any credit guarantee? . . .'

'. . . When you've got your degree, you must get married,

and then the both of you must take over the business. Your mother isn't any use . . .'

'. . . Your mother won't get out of her chair all day long . . . She's becoming impossible to manage . . . You ought to come home . . .'

'. . . The Goldstein boy, who got back two weeks ago, says you're not enrolled at the University of Paris. I told him he was wrong and . . .'

'. . . Your mother's had her legs tapped and she . . .'

'. . . You've been seen in Paris in unsuitable company, I want to know what is going on . . .'

'. . . I've had more unpleasant information about you. As soon as business permits, I shall come and see for myself . . .'

'. . . If it wasn't for your mother, who does not want to be left alone and who according to the doctor will not recover, I would be coming to get you right now. I order you to come home . . .'

'. . . I'm sending you five hundred zloty for the fare . . .'

'. . . If you are not home within a month I will curse you . . .'

Then more on the mother's legs. Then what a Jewish student on a home visit to Vilna told them about her bachelor life in Paris.

'. . . Unless you come home straight away I want nothing more to do with you . . .'

Then the final letter:

'. . . How have you managed for a whole year since I stopped sending you any money? Your mother is very upset. She says it is all my fault . . .'

Detective Chief Inspector Maigret did not smile once. He put the papers in his drawer and locked it, drafted a few telegrams and then went down to the police cells.

Anna Gorskin had spent the night in the common room. But Maigret had at last ordered them to put her in a private cell, and he went and peered at her through the grating in the door. Anna was sitting on the stool. She didn't jump but slowly turned her face towards the hatch, looked straight at Maigret and sneered at him.

He went into the cell and stood there looking at Anna for quite a while. He realized that there was no point trying to be clever or asking those oblique questions that sometimes prompt an inadvertent admission of guilt.

He just grunted:

'Anything to confess?'

'I admit nothing!'

'Do you still deny killing Mortimer?'

'I admit nothing!'

'Do you deny having bought grey clothes for your accomplice?'

'I admit nothing!'

'Do you deny having them taken up to his room at the Majestic together with a letter in which you declared you were going to kill Mortimer and also made an appointment to meet outside the hotel?'

'I admit nothing!'

'What were you doing at the Majestic?'

'I was looking for Madame Goldstein.'

'There's nobody of that name at the hotel.'

'I was unaware of that . . .'

'So why were you running away with a gun in your hand when I came across you?'

'In the first floor corridor I saw a man fire at someone and then drop his gun on the floor. I picked it up off the floor in case he decided to fire it at me. I was running to raise the alarm . . .'

'Had you ever set eyes on Mortimer?'

'No . . .'

'But he went to your lodgings in Rue du Roi-de-Sicile.'

'There are sixty tenants in the building.'

'Do you know Pietr the Latvian, or Oswald Oppenheim?'

'No . . .'

'That does not hold water . . .'

'*I don't give a damn!*'

'We'll find the salesman who brought up the grey suit.'

'Go ahead!'

'I've told your father, in Vilna . . .'

For the first time she tensed up. But she put on a grin straight away:

'If you want him to make the effort then you'd better send him the fare . . .'

Maigret didn't rise to the bait, but just carried on watching her – with interest, but also with some sympathy. You couldn't deny she had guts!

On first reading, her statement seemed insubstantial. The facts seemed to speak for themselves. But that's exactly the kind of situation where the police often lack sufficient solid evidence with which to confound the suspect's denials.

And in this case, they had no evidence at all! The revolver hadn't been supplied by any of the gunsmiths in Paris, so there was no way of proving it belonged to Anna Gorskin. Second: she'd been at the Majestic at the time of the murder, but it's not forbidden to walk in and around large hotels of that kind as if they were public spaces. Third: she claimed she'd been looking for someone, and that couldn't be ruled out.

Nobody had seen her pull the trigger. Nothing remained of the letter that Pietr had burned.

Circumstantial evidence? There was a ton of it. But juries don't reach a verdict on circumstantial evidence alone. They're wary of even the clearest proof for fear of making a judicial error, the ghost that defence lawyers are forever parading in front of them.

Maigret played his last card.

'Pietr's been seen in Fécamp . . .'

That got the response he wanted. Anna Gorskin shuddered. But she told herself he was lying, so she got a grip on herself and didn't rise to the bait.

'So what?'

'We have an anonymous letter – we're checking it out right now – that says he's hiding in a villa with someone called Swaan . . .'

Anna glanced up at him with her dark eyes. She looked grave, almost tragic.

Maigret was looking without thinking at Anna Gorskin's ankles and noticed that, as her mother feared, the young woman already had dropsy. Her scalp was visible through her thinning hair, which was in a mess. Her black dress was dirty. And there was a distinct shadow on her upper lip.

All the same she was a good-looking woman, in a common, feral way. Sitting sideways on the stool, or rather huddling up in self-defence, she fired daggers from her eyes as she scowled at the inspector.

'If you know all that already, why bother to ask me? . . .'

Her eyes flashed, and she added with an offensive laugh:

'Unless you're afraid of bringing *her* down too! . . . I'm right, aren't I? . . . Ha! Ha! . . . I don't matter . . . I'm just a foreigner . . . A ghetto girl living from hand to mouth . . . But she's different! . . . Oh well . . .'

She was going to talk. Jealousy had done it. Maigret sensed that he might scare her off if he seemed too interested, so he put on a nonchalant air and looked away. But she screamed out:

'Well . . . You get nothing! Did you hear me? Buzz off and leave me alone. I told you already, you get nothing! . . . Not a thing!'

She threw herself to the floor in a way that could not have been forestalled even by men well acquainted with this kind of woman. She was having a fit of hysterics! Her face was all distorted, her arms and legs were writhing on the floor, and her body juddered with muscular spasms.

What had been a beautiful woman was now a hideous hag tearing whole tufts of hair off her head with no thought for the pain.

Maigret wasn't alarmed, he'd seen a hundred fits of this kind already. He picked the water jug off the floor. It was empty. He called a guard:

'Fill this up, quickly.'

Within minutes he'd poured cold water over the woman's face. She gasped, greedily opened her mouth, looked at Maigret without knowing who he was, then fell into a deep slumber. Now and again small spasms ran across the surface of her body.

Maigret let down the bed, which had been raised against the wall as required by regulations, smoothed out the wafer-thin mattress and with great effort picked up Anna Gorskin and laid her on the bed.

He did all that without the slightest resentment, with a gentleness you'd never think he was capable of. He pulled the unhappy woman's dress down over her knees, took her pulse and watched over her for a long while.

In this light she had the look of a worn-out woman of thirty-five. Her forehead was full of tiny wrinkles you couldn't usually see. Conversely her chubby hands, with cheap varnish clumsily painted on her nails, had a delicate shape.

Maigret filled his pipe slowly with his index finger, like a man not sure what to do next. For a while he paced up and down the cell, with its door still ajar.

Suddenly he turned around, for he could hardly believe his eyes.

Anna Gorskin had just pulled the blanket up over her face. She was just a shapeless lump underneath the ugly grey cotton cover. A lump that was heaving up and down in staccato. If you strained your ear you could hear her muffled sobs.

Maigret went out noiselessly, shut the door behind him, went past the guard then, when he had gone ten metres further on, came back on his tracks.

'Have her meals sent over from Brasserie Dauphine!' he blurted out, grumpily.

15. Two Telegrams

Maigret read them aloud to Monsieur Coméliau, the examining magistrate, who had a bored expression on his face.

The first was a wire from Mrs Mortimer-Levingston in response to the message informing her of her husband's murder.

Berlin. Hotel Modern. Am sick with a high temperature, cannot travel. Stones will deal with it.

Maigret smiled sourly.

'Do you see? Here's the message from Wilhelmstrasse, for contrast. It's in IPC, I'll translate it for you:

Mrs Mortimer arrived air, staying Hotel Modern, Berlin. Found message Paris on return from theatre. Took to bed and called American medic Pelgrad. Doctor claims confidentiality privilege. Query bring in second opinion? Hotel staff not aware any symptoms.

'As you can see, your honour, the lady is not keen to be questioned by French police. Mind you, I'm not claiming she's an accomplice. Quite the opposite, in fact. I'm sure Mortimer hid ninety-nine per cent of his activities from her. He wasn't the kind of man to trust a women, especially not his wife. But the bottom line is that she passed on a message one evening at Pickwick's Bar to a professional dancer who's now on ice in the morgue . . . That might be the only time that Mortimer used her, out of sheer necessity . . .'

'What about Stones?' the magistrate inquired.

'Mortimer's principal secretary. He was in charge of communications between the boss and his various businesses. At the time of the murder he'd been in London for a week, staying at the Victoria Hotel. I was careful to keep him out of the picture. But I called Scotland Yard and asked them to check the man out. Please note that when the English police turned up at the Victoria, news of Mortimer's death hadn't been released in the country, though it may have reached the news desks. Nonetheless the bird had flown. Stones did a bunk a few minutes before the police got there . . .'

The magistrate surveyed the pile of letters and telegrams cluttering his desk with a gloomy look on his face.

'Do you think we should foster the rumour that it was a love murder?' Coméliau asked, without conviction.

'I think that would be wise. Otherwise you'll set off a stock market panic and ruin a number of honourable businesses – first and foremost, those French companies that Mortimer had just bailed out.'

'Obviously, but . . .'

'Hang on a moment! The US Embassy will want proof . . . And you haven't got any! . . . And nor do I . . .'

The magistrate wiped his glasses.

'And the consequence is . . . ?'

'None . . . I'm waiting for news from Dufour, who's been in Fécamp since yesterday . . . Give Mortimer a fine funeral . . . Doesn't matter. With speeches and official delegations.'

The magistrate had been looking at Maigret with curiosity for the last few minutes.

'You look funny . . .' he said suddenly.

The inspector smiled and put on a confidential air:

'It's morphine!' he said.

'Eh? . . .'

'Don't worry! I'm not hooked on it yet! Just a little injection in my chest . . . The medics want to remove two of my ribs, they say it's absolutely necessary . . . But it's a huge job! . . . I'll have to go into a clinic and stay there for God knows how many weeks . . . I asked for sixty hours' stay of execution . . . The worst outcome would be losing a third rib . . . Two more than Adam! . . . That's all! Now you're treating this like a tragedy as well . . . It's obvious you haven't gone over the pros and cons with Professor Cochet, who's fiddled about with the innards of almost all the world's kings and masters . . . He'd have told you as he told me that there are thousands of people missing all sorts of bits and pieces in their bodies . . . Take the Czech premier . . . Cochet removed one of his kidneys . . . I saw it . . . He showed me all sorts of things, lungs, stomachs . . . And the people who had them before are still around, all over the world, getting on with their lives . . .'

He checked the time on his wristwatch, muttering:

'Come on, Dufour! . . .'

He was now looking serious again. The air in the magistrate's office was blue with the smoke from Maigret's pipe. The inspector perched on the edge of the desk; he had made himself quite at home. After a pause:

'I think I'd better pop down to Fécamp myself!' he sighed. 'There's a train in an hour . . .'

'Nasty business!' Coméliau said, as if to bring the case to an end, pushing the file away.

Maigret was lost in contemplation of the pall of smoke all around him. The only noise that broke the silence, or rather gave it a rhythm, was the gurgling of his pipe.

'Look at this photograph,' he said all of a sudden.

He held out the Pskov photograph showing the tailor's white-gabled house, the hoist, the six steps and the seated mother, with the father posing and the two lads in their embroidered sailor collar shirts.

'That's in Russia! I had to look it up in an atlas. Not far from the Baltic Sea. There are several small countries in those parts: Estonia, Lithuania, Latvia . . . With Poland and Russia surrounding them. The national borders don't match ethnic boundaries. From one village to the next you change language. And on top of that you've got Jews spread all over, constituting a separate race. And besides that, there are the communists! There are border wars going on all the time! And the armies of the ultra-nationalists . . . People live on pine-cones in the woods. The poor over there are poorer than anywhere else. Some of them die of cold and hunger. There are intellectuals defending German culture, others defending Slavic culture, and still others defending local customs and ancient dialects . . . Some of the peasants have the look of Lapps or Kalmyks, others are tall and blond, and then you've got mixed-race Jews who eat garlic and slaughter livestock their own special way . . .'

Maigret took the photograph back from the magistrate, who hadn't seemed very interested in it.

'What odd little boys!' was his only comment.

Maigret handed it back to the magistrate and asked:

'Can you tell me which of the two I'm looking for?'

Three-quarters of an hour remained before the train left. Magistrate Coméliau studied in turn the boy who seemed to be challenging the photographer and his brother, who could be turning towards the other one to ask for his advice.

'Photographs like that speak volumes!' Maigret continued. 'It makes you wonder why their parents and their teachers who saw them like that didn't guess right off what lay in store for these characters. Look closely at the father . . . He was killed in a riot one evening when the nationalists were fighting communists in the streets . . . He wasn't on either side . . . He'd just gone out to get a loaf of bread . . . I got the story by sheer chance from the landlord of the Roi de Sicile, who comes from Pskov . . . The mother's still alive and lives in the same house. On Sundays she puts on national dress, with a tall hat that comes down on the sides . . . And the boys . . .'

Maigret stopped. His voice changed entirely.

'Mortimer was born on a farm in Ohio and started out selling shoelaces in San Francisco. Anna Gorskin, who was born in Odessa, spent her early years in Vilna. Mrs Mortimer, lastly, is a Scot who emigrated to Florida when still a child. And the whole lot have ended up a stone's throw from Notre-Dame-de-Paris. Whereas I'm the son of a gamekeeper on a Loire Valley estate that goes back centuries.'

He looked at his watch again and pointed to the boy in the photograph who was staring admiringly at his brother.

'What I've got to do now is lay my hands on that boy there!'

He emptied his pipe into the coal bucket and almost began filling up the stove, out of habit.

A few minutes later Magistrate Coméliau was wiping his gold-rimmed spectacles and saying to his clerk:

'Don't you find Maigret changed? I though he was . . . how should I put it . . . rather excited . . . rather . . .'

He couldn't find the right word, and then cut to the main point:

'What the hell are all these foreigners doing here?'

Then he abruptly pulled over the Mortimer file and began to dictate:

'Take this down: *In the year nineteen . . .*'

Inspector Dufour was in the very same nook in the wall where Maigret had kept watch on the man in the trench-coat one stormy day, because it was the only niche to be found in the steep alleyway that led first to the handful of villas on the cliff and then turned into a track that petered out in a grazed meadow.

Dufour was wearing black spats, a short, belted cloak and a sailor's cap, like everyone else in these parts. He must have acquired it on arrival at Fécamp.

'So? . . .' Maigret asked as he came upon him in the dark.

'All going fine, chief.'

He found that rather worrying.

'What's going fine?'

'The man hasn't come in or gone out . . . If he got to Fécamp before me and went to the villa, then that's where he is . . .'

'Give me the whole story, in detail.'

'Yesterday morning, nothing to report. The maid went to market. In the evening I had Detective Bornier relieve me. Nobody in or out all night long. Lights out at ten . . .'

'Next?'

'I returned to my post this morning, and Bornier went to bed . . . He'll come back and relieve me . . . Around nine, same as yesterday, the maid went off to the market . . . About half an hour ago a young lady came out . . . She'll be back shortly . . . I guess she's gone to call on someone . . .'

Maigret kept quiet. He realized how far the surveillance fell short of the mark. But how many men would he need to make a job like this completely watertight?

To keep the villa under permanent observation he would need at least three men. Then he'd need a detective to tail the maid, and another one for the 'young lady', as Dufour called her!

'She's been gone thirty minutes?'

'Yes . . . Look! Here comes Bornier . . . My turn for a meal break . . . I've only had a sandwich all day and my feet are freezing . . .'

'Off you go . . .'

Detective Bornier was a young man just starting out with the Flying Squad.

'I met Madame Swaan . . .' he said.

'Where? When?'

'At the dockside . . . Just now . . . She was going towards the outer pier . . .'

'On her own?'

'Yes, alone. I thought of tailing her . . . But then I remembered Dufour was expecting me . . . The pier's a dead end, so she can't get very far . . .'

'What was she wearing?'

'A dark coat . . . I didn't pay attention . . .'

'Can I go now?' Dufour asked.

'I told you already . . .'

'If anything comes up, you will let me know, won't you? . . . All you have to do is ring on the hotel bell three times in a row . . .'

What an idiot! Maigret was barely listening. He told Bornier: 'You stay here . . .' and then took off quite abruptly for the Swaans' villa, where he tugged at the bell-pull at the gate so hard that it nearly came off. He could see light on the ground floor, in the room he now knew to be the dining room.

Nobody came for five minutes, so he climbed over the low wall, got to the front door, and banged on it with his fist.

From inside a terrified voice wailed:

'Who's there?'

He could hear children crying as well.

'Police! Open up!'

There was a pause and the sound of scuffling feet.

'Open up! Get a move on!'

The hallway was unlit, but as he went in Maigret made out a white rectangle that could only be the maid's apron.

'Madame Swaan?'

At that point a door swung open and he saw the little girl he'd noticed on his first visit. The maid stood stock still with her back to the wall. You could tell she was rigid with fright.

'Who did you see this morning?'

'Officer, I swear I . . .'

She collapsed in tears.

'I swear . . . I swear . . .'

'Was it Captain Swaan?'

'No! . . . I . . . It was . . . madame's . . . brother-in-law . . . He gave me a letter to give to madame . . .'

'Where was he?'

'Opposite the butcher's . . . He was waiting for me there
. . .'

'Was that the first time he's asked you to do jobs of that
kind?'

'Yes, the first time . . . I never saw him before except in
this house.'

' . . . Do you know where he planned to join up with
Madame Swaan?'

'I don't know anything! . . . Madame has been in a nervous state all day . . . She asked me questions as well. She
wanted to know how he looked . . . I told her the truth, I
said he looked like he was on the edge . . . He scared me
when he came up close.'

Maigret rushed out without closing the door behind
him.

16. On the Rocks

Detective Bornier, a newcomer to the Squad, was quite horrified to see the chief run straight past, brushing him as he went without a word of apology and leaving the front door of the villa wide open. Twice he called out:

'Inspector Maigret! Inspector, sir!'

But Maigret did not turn back. He only slowed down a few minutes later, when he got to Rue d'Étretat, where there were some passers-by, then he turned to the right, sploshed through the mud at the dockside and started running again towards the outer pier.

He'd only gone 100 metres when he made out the figure of a woman. He switched to the other side so as to get nearer to her. There was a trawler with an acetylene lamp up in the rigging – that meant it was unloading its catch.

He stopped so as to allow the woman to reach the pool of light and he saw it was the face of Madame Swaan, in great distress. She was rolling her eyes and walking with a hurried and clumsy tread, as if she were hopping over deep ruts and by some miracle not falling into them.

The inspector was ready to tackle her and had already started to walk over. But the long black line of the deserted pier stretching out into the dark, with waves breaking over both sides, caught his eye. He rushed towards it. Beyond the trawler there wasn't a soul to be seen. The green and red flare of the harbour passage light cut through the night. The light was set on the rocks and every fifteen seconds it flashed over a wide stretch of water then lit up the outer cliff, which blinked on and off like a ghost.

Maigret stumbled over capstans as he found his way onto the pontoon, in the noise of crashing waves.

He strained his eyes to see in the dark. A ship's siren wailed a request to be let out of the lock.

In front of him was the blank and noisy sea. Behind him, the town with its shops and slippery pavements.

He strode on quickly, stopping at intervals to peer into the darkness, with increasing anxiety.

He didn't know the terrain and took what he thought was a short cut. The walkway on stilts led him to the foot of a lighthouse where there were three black cannonballs, which he counted without thinking why. Further on, he leaned over the railing and looked down on great pools of white foam settling between outcrops of rock.

The wind blew his hat off his head. He chased after it but couldn't stop it from falling into the sea. Seagulls screeched overhead, and every now and again he could make out a white wing flapping against the black sky.

Maybe Madame Swaan had found nobody waiting for her at the appointed place. Maybe her assignation had had time to get away? Maybe he was dead.

Maigret was hopping up and down, he was sure that every second counted.

He reached the green light and went round the steel platform on which it stood.

Nobody there! Waves raised their crests high, tottered, crashed down and retreated from the foamy hollow before renewing their attack on the breakwater. The sound of grinding shingle reached his ears in bursts. He could make out the vague outline of the deserted Casino.

Maigret was looking for a man!

He turned back and wandered along the shore among stones that in the dark all looked like huge potatoes. He was down at the waterline. Sea spray hit his face.

That was when he realized it was low tide, and that the pier stood on black rocks with swirling seawater in the hollows between them.

It was a complete miracle that he caught sight of the man. At first glance he looked like an inanimate object, just a blur among other blurry shapes in the dark.

He strained his eyes to see. It was something on the outermost rock, where breakers rose to their proudest height before collapsing into thousands of droplets.

But it was alive.

To get there Maigret had to slither through the struts holding up the walkway he'd run along a few minutes previously.

The rocks underfoot were covered in seaweed and Maigret's soles kept slipping and sliding. Hissing sounds came from all around – crabs fleeing in their hundreds, or air bubbles bursting, algae popping, mussels quivering on the wooden beams they'd colonized halfway to the top.

At one point Maigret lost his footing, plunging knee-deep into a rock pool.

He'd lost sight of the man but he knew he was going

in the right direction. Whoever it was must have got to his spot when the tide had been even lower, because Inspector Maigret found himself held back by a pool that was now over two metres wide. He tested the depth with his right foot and nearly tipped right over. In the end he got across by hanging on to the ironwork supporting the stilts.

These are times when it's better not to be watched. You try out movements you've not been trained to do. You get them wrong every time, like a clumsy acrobat. But even so you make headway, pushed forwards by your own mass, so to speak. You fall and you get up again. There's no skill and no grace to it, but you splash on nonetheless.

Maigret got a cut in his cheek but he could never work out whether it was from a fall on the rocks or a graze from a nail in one of the beams.

He caught sight of the man again but wondered if he was seeing things: the man was so perfectly still that he could have been one of those rocks that from afar take on the shape of a human being.

He got to the point where he had water slapping about between his legs. Maigret was not the sea-going type.

He couldn't help himself but hurry on forwards.

At last he reached the outcrop where the man was sitting. He was one metre higher than his target, and three or four metres away.

He didn't think of getting his gun out, but insofar as the terrain allowed it he tiptoed forwards, knocking stones down into the water, whose roar covered the noise.

Then, suddenly, without transition, he pounced on the

stationary figure, put his neck in an arm-lock and pulled him down backwards.

The pair of them almost slipped and disappeared into one of the big rollers that break over those rocks. They were spared by sheer chance.

Any attempt to repeat the exploit would surely have ended in disaster.

The man hadn't seen who was attacking him, and he slithered like a snake. He could not free his head, but he wriggled with what must surely be counted in those circumstances as superhuman agility.

Maigret didn't want to strangle him. He was only trying to overpower him. He'd hooked one of his feet behind a stilt, and that foot was all that was keeping the pair of them from falling off.

His opponent didn't struggle for long. He'd only fought out of spontaneous reaction, like an animal.

As soon as he'd had time to think, at any rate once he'd seen it was Maigret, whose face was right next to his, he stopped moving.

He blinked his eyes to indicate surrender and when his neck was freed, he nodded towards the shifting and mountainous sea and blurted out in a still unsteady voice:

'Watch out . . .'

'Would you like to talk, Hans Johannson?'

Maigret was hanging on to a piece of slippery seaweed by his fingernails. When it was all over he confessed that at this precise moment his opponent could have easily kicked him into the water. It was only a second, but Johannson, squatting beside the last stilt of the pier, didn't take advantage of it. Later still, Maigret confessed with great honesty that he had had to hang on to his prisoner's foot to haul himself back up the slope.

Then the two of them began the return journey, without a word between them. The tide had risen further. A few metres from shore they were cut off by the same rock pool that had blocked the inspector on his way out, but it was deeper now.

Pietr went down first, stumbled when he was three metres in, slipped over, coughed up seawater, then stood up. It was only waist-deep. Maigret plunged in. At one point he closed his eyes as he felt he couldn't keep the huge weight of his body above the surface any more. But the two of them eventually found themselves dripping on the pebbles of the shore.

'Did she talk?' Pietr asked in a voice so blank that it seemed to be devoid of anything that might still harbour a will to live.

Maigret was entitled to lie but instead he declared:

'She told me nothing . . . But I know . . .'

They could not stay where they were. The wind was turning their wet clothes into an ice-jacket. Pietr's teeth started chattering. Even in the faint moonlight Maigret could see that the man's lips had turned blue.

He'd lost his moustache. He had the worried face of Fyodor Yurevich, the look of the little boy in Pskov gazing at his brother. But though his eyes were the same cloudy grey as before, they now stared with a harsh and unyielding gaze.

A three-quarters turn to the right would allow them to see the cliff and the two or three lights that twinkled on it. One of them came from Madame Swaan's villa.

Each time the beam of the harbour light went round,

you caught a glimpse of the roof that shielded Madame Swaan, the two children and the frightened maid.

'Come on . . .' Maigret said.

'To the police station?'

Maigret sounded resigned, or rather, indifferent.

'No . . .'

He was familiar with one of the harbour-side hotels, Chez Léon, where he'd noticed an entrance that was used only in the summer, for the handful of holiday-makers who spend the season by the sea at Fécamp. The entrance gave onto a room that was turned into a fairly grand dining room in high season. In winter, though, sailors were happy to drink and eat oysters and herring in the main bar.

That was the door Maigret used. He crossed the unlit room with his prisoner and found himself in the kitchen. A maid screamed in stupefaction.

'Call the *patron* . . .'

She stood still and yelled:

'Monsieur Léon! . . . Monsieur Léon! . . .'

'Give me a room . . .' the inspector said when Léon came in.

'Monsieur Maigret! . . . But you're soaking! . . . Did you? . . .'

'A room, quickly! . . .'

'There's no fire made up in any of the rooms! . . . And a hot-water bottle will never . . .'

'Don't you have a pair of bathrobes?'

'Of course . . . My own . . . but . . .'

He was shorter than the inspector by three heads!

'Bring them down.'

They climbed a steep staircase with quaint bends in it. The room was decent. Monsieur Léon closed the shutters himself before suggesting:

'Hot toddy, right? . . . Full strength! . . .'

'Good idea . . . But get those bathrobes first . . .'

Maigret realized he was falling ill again, from the cold. The injured side of his chest felt like a block of ice.

For a few minutes he and his prisoner got on like roommates. They got undressed. Monsieur Léon handed them his two bathrobes by stretching his arm around the door when it was ajar.

'I'll have the larger one,' the inspector said.

Pietr compared them for size. As he handed over the larger one to Maigret he noticed the wet bandage, and a nervous twitch broke out on his face.

'Is it serious?'

'Two or three ribs that'll have to be removed sooner or later . . .'

A silence ensued. It was broken by Monsieur Léon, who shouted from the other side of the door:

'Everything all right? . . .'

'Come in!'

Maigret's bathrobe barely covered his knees, leaving his thick, hairy calves for all to see.

Pietr, on the contrary, who was slim and pale with fair hair and feminine ankles, looked like a stylish clown.

'The toddy's on its way! I'll get your clothes dried, yes?'

Monsieur Léon gathered up the two soggy and dripping heaps on the floor and then shouted down from the top of the stairs:

'Come on then, Henriette . . . Where's that toddy?'

Then he tracked back to the bedroom and gave this advice:

'Don't talk too loud in here . . . There's a travelling salesman from Le Havre in the room next door . . . He's catching the 5 a.m. train . . .'

17. *And a Bottle of Rum*

It would be an exaggeration to say that in most criminal inquiries cordial relations arise between the police and the person they are trying to corner into a confession. All the same, they almost always become close to some degree (unless the suspect is just a glowering brute). That must be because for weeks and sometimes months on end the police and the suspect do nothing but think about each other.

The investigator strives to know all he can about the suspect's past, seeks to reconstitute his thinking and to foresee his reactions.

Both sides have high stakes in the game. When they sit down to a match, they do so in circumstances that are dramatic enough to strip away the veneer of polite indifference that passes for human relations in everyday life.

There have been cases of detectives who'd taken a lot of trouble to put a criminal behind bars growing fond of the culprit, to the extent of visiting him in prison and offering emotional support up to the moment of execution.

That partly explains the attitude that the two men adopted once they were alone in the hotel bedroom. The hotelier had brought up a portable charcoal stove, and a kettle was whistling on the hob. Beside it stood two glasses, a dish of sugar cubes and a tall bottle of rum.

Both men were cold. They huddled in their borrowed

dressing gowns and leaned as close as they could to the little stove, which wasn't nearly strong enough to warm them up.

They were as casual with each other as if they were stuck in a dorm-room or a barracks, with the informality that arises between men only when social proprieties have become temporarily irrelevant.

In fact, it might have been simply because they were cold. Or more likely because of the weariness that overcame them at the same moment.

It was over! No words were needed to say that.

So each slumped into a chair and gazed at the blue enamel cooking stove that linked them together.

The Latvian was the one who took the bottle of rum and expertly mixed the toddy.

After taking a few sips, Maigret asked:

'Did you mean to kill her?'

The reply came straight away and it was just as straightforward:

'I couldn't do it.'

His face was all screwed up with nervous tics that gave the man no rest. His eyelids would bat up and down, his lips would go into spasms, his nostrils would twitch. The determined and intelligent face of Pietr started to dissolve into the face of Fyodor, the intensely agitated Russian vagrant. Maigret didn't bother to watch.

That's why he didn't realize that his opponent kept on taking the bottle of rum, filling his glass, and drinking it down. His eyes were beginning to shine.

'Was she married to Pietr? . . . He was the same as Olaf Swaan, wasn't he?'

The man from Pskov couldn't sit still, so he got up, looked for a packet of cigarettes but couldn't find any and seemed put out by that. As he came back past the table with the stove he poured himself some more rum.

'That's not the right starting point!' he said.

Then he looked Maigret straight in the eye:

'In a nutshell: you know the almost whole story already, don't you?'

'The two brothers of Pskov . . . Twins, I suppose? You're Hans, the one who was looking lovingly and tamely at the other one . . .'

'Even when we were kids he found it amusing to treat me as his servant . . . Not just between ourselves, but in front of classmates . . . He didn't call me his servant – he said: slave . . . He'd noticed I liked that . . . Because I did like it, I still don't know why . . . He was everything to me . . . I'd have got myself killed for his sake . . . When, later on . . .'

'Later on, when?'

He froze up. His eyelids flapped up and down. A swig of rum. Then he shrugged as if to say, what the hell. Then, controlling himself:

'When later on I came to love a woman, I don't think I was capable of any greater devotion . . . Probably less! I loved Pietr like . . . I can't find the word! . . . I got into fights with classmates who wouldn't grant that he was better than any of them, and as I was the least muscular boy in my class I got beaten up, and I got a kick out of it.'

'That kind of domination isn't uncommon between twins,' Maigret commented as he made himself a second glass of toddy. 'May I just take a moment?' He went to the door and called down to Léon to bring up the pipe he'd left in his clothes, together with some tobacco. Hans added:

'Can I have some cigarettes, do you mind?'

'And some cigarettes, Léon . . . Gauloises!'

He sat down again. They said nothing until the maid had brought up the supplies and withdrawn.

'You were both students at the University of Tartu . . .' Maigret resumed.

The other man couldn't sit still or stop moving around. He nibbled the end of his cigarette as he smoked and spat out scraps of tobacco, jiggled from side to side, picked up a vase from the mantelpiece and put it down somewhere else, and got more and more excited as he talked.

'Yes, that's where it all began! My brother was top of the class. All the professors paid attention to him. Students came under his spell. So although he was one of the youngest, he was made Captain of Ugala.

'We drank lots of beer in the taverns. I did, especially! I don't know why I started drinking so young. I had no special reason. In a word, I've been a drinker all my life.

'I think it was mainly because after a few glasses I could imagine a world to my own liking in which I would play a splendid part . . .

'Pietr was very hard on me. He called me a "dirty Russian". You can't know what that means. Our maternal grandmother was Russian. But in our part of the world, especially in the post-war years, Russians were treated as drunken dreamers and layabouts.

'At that time the communists were stoking up riots. My brother led the Ugala Fraternity. They went to get weapons from a barracks and faced the communists head-on in the centre of town.

'I was scared . . . It wasn't my fault . . . I was frightened
. . . I couldn't use my legs . . . I stayed in the tavern with
the shutters closed and drank my way through the whole
thing.

'I thought I was destined to become a great playwright,
like Chekhov. I knew all his plays by heart. Pietr just
laughed at me.

'"You . . . You'll never make it!" he said.

'The disturbances and riots lasted a whole year, turning
life upside down. The army wasn't up to maintaining
order, so citizens got together in vigilante groups to defend
the town.

'My brother, Captain of the Ugala Fraternity, became
an important person, and he was taken seriously by people
of substance. He didn't yet have any hair on his lip, but he
was already being talked about as a potential leader of
Free Estonia.

'But calm returned, and then a scandal erupted that had
to be hushed up. When the accounts of the Ugala Club
were done, it turned out that Pietr had used the group
mainly to enrich himself.

'He was on several of the subcommittees and he'd fiddled all the books.

'He had to leave the country. He went to Berlin and
wrote to ask me to join him there.

'That's where the two of us began.'

Maigret watched the man's face. It was too agitated by half.

'Which of you was the forger?'

'Pietr taught me how to mimic anybody's handwriting,
and made me take a course in chemistry . . . I lived in a
little room, and he gave me 200 marks a week to live on

. . . But he soon bought himself a car, to take girls out for rides . . .

'Mainly, we doctored cheques . . . I could turn a cheque for ten marks into a cheque for ten thousand, and Pietr would cash it in Switzerland or Holland or even, one time, in Spain . . .

'I was drinking heavily. He despised me and treated me spitefully. One day I nearly got him caught accidentally, because one of my forgeries wasn't quite up to the mark.

'He beat me with his walking stick . . .

'And I said nothing! I still looked up to him . . . I don't know why . . . He impressed everyone, actually . . . At one point, if he'd wanted to, he could have married the daughter of a Reichsminister . . .

'Because of the dud forgery we had to get to France. To begin with I lived in Rue de l'École-de-Médecine . . .

'Pietr wasn't on his own. He'd linked up with several international gangs . . . He travelled abroad a lot and he used me less and less. Only occasionally, for forgeries, because I'd got very good at that . . .

'He gave me small amounts of money. He always said: "You'll never do more than drink, you filthy Russian!" . . .

'One day he told me he was going to America for a huge deal which would make him super-rich. He ordered me to go live in the country because I'd already been picked up several times in Paris by the immigration authorities. "All I'm asking is for you to lie low! . . . Not too much to ask, is it?" But he also asked me to supply him with a set of false passports, which I did.'

'And that's how you met the woman who became Madame Swaan . . .'

'Her name was Berthe . . .'

A pause. The man's Adam's apple was bouncing up and down. Then he blurted it all out:

'You can't imagine how much I wanted to *be something*! She was the cashier at the hotel where I was staying . . . She saw me coming back drunk every night . . . She would scold me . . .

'She was very young, but a serious person. She made me think of having a house and children . . .

'One evening she was lecturing me when I wasn't too drunk. I wept in her arms and I think I promised I would start over and become a new man.

'I think I would have kept my word. I was sick of everything! I'd had enough of the low life! . . .

'It lasted almost a month . . . Look! It was stupid . . . On Sundays we went to the bandstand together . . . It was autumn . . . We would walk back by way of the harbour and look at the boats . . .

'We didn't talk about love . . . She said she was my chum . . . But I knew that one day . . .

'That's right! One day my brother did come back. He needed me right away . . . He had a whole suitcase of cheques that needed doctoring . . . It was hard to imagine how he'd got hold of so many! . . . They were drawn on all the major banks in the world . . .

'He'd become a merchant seaman for the time being under the alias of Olaf Swaan . . . He stayed at my hotel . . . While I sweated over the cheques for weeks on end – doctoring cheques is tricky work! – he toured the Channel ports looking for boats to buy . . .

'His new business was booming. He told me he'd done a deal with a leading American financier, who would obviously be kept at arm's length from the scam.

'The aim was to get all the main international gangs to pull together.

'The bootleggers had already agreed to cooperate. Now they needed small boats to smuggle the alcohol . . .

'Do I need to tell you the rest? Pietr had cut off supplies of drink, to make me work harder . . . I lived alone in my little room with weaver's glasses, acids, pens and inks of every kind. I even had a portable printing press . . .

'One day I went into my brother's room without knocking. He had Berthe in his arms . . .'

He grabbed the almost empty bottle and poured the last dregs down his throat.

'I walked out,' he concluded in a peculiar tone. 'I had no option. I walked out . . . I got on a train . . . I tottered round every bar in Paris for days on end . . . and washed up in Rue du Roi-de-Sicile, dead drunk and sick as a dog!'

18. Hans at Home

'I suppose I can only make women feel sorry for me. When I woke up there was a Jewish girl taking care of me . . . She got the idea she should stop me drinking, just like the last one! . . . And she treated me like I was a child, as well! . . .'

He laughed. His eyes were misty. His restless fidgeting and twitching was exhausting to watch.

'Only this girl stuck it out. As for Pietr . . . I guess our being twins isn't insignificant, and we do have things in common . . .

'I told you he could have married a German society figure . . . Well, he didn't! He married Berthe, some while later, when she'd changed job and was working in Fécamp . . . He never told her the truth . . . I can see why not! . . . He needed a quiet, neat little place of his own . . . He had children with her! . . .'

That seemed to be more than he could bear. His voice broke. Real tears came to his eyes but they dried up straight away: maybe his eyelids were so hot they just evaporated.

'Right up to this morning she really believed she'd married the master of an ocean-going vessel . . . He would turn up now and again and spend a weekend or a month with her and the kids . . . Meanwhile, I was stuck with the other woman . . . with Anna . . . It's a mystery why she loved me . . . But she did love me, no doubt about that . . . So I treated her the way my brother had always treated me . . . I threw insults at her . . . I was constantly humiliating her . . .

'When I got drunk, she would weep . . . So I drank *on purpose* . . . I even took opium and other kinds of crap . . . *On purpose* . . . Then I would get ill, and she would look after me for weeks on end . . . I was turning into a wreck . . .'

He waved at his own body with an expression of disgust. Then he wheedled:

'Could you get me something to drink?'

Maigret hesitated only briefly, then went to the landing:

'*Patron*, send up some rum!' he shouted.

The man from Pskov didn't say thank you.

'I used to run away now and again, to Fécamp, where I prowled around the villa where Berthe lived . . . I remember her walking her first baby in the pram . . . Pietr had had to tell her I was his brother, because we looked so similar . . . Then I got an idea. When we were kids I'd learned to imitate Pietr, out of admiration . . . Anyway, one day, with all those dark thoughts in my mind, I went down to Fécamp dressed in clothes like his . . .

'The maid fell for it . . . As I went into the house the kid came up to me and cried "Papa!" . . . What a fool I was! I ran away! But all the same it stuck in my mind . . .

'From time to time Pietr made appointments to see me . . . He needed me to forge things for him . . . And I said yes! Why? I hated him, but I was under his thumb . . . He was swimming in money, swanning around in five-star hotels and high society . . .

'He was caught twice, but he got off both times . . .

'I was never involved in what he was up to, but you must have seen through it as I did. When he'd been working on his own or with just a handful of accomplices, he only did things on a modest scale . . . But then Mortimer, whom I met only recently, got him in his sights . . . My brother had skills, cheek and maybe a touch of genius. Mortimer had scope and a rock-solid reputation the world over . . . Pietr's job was to get the top crooks to work in cahoots on Mortimer's behalf and to set up the scams. Mortimer was the banker . . .

'I didn't give a damn . . . As my brother had told me when I was a student at Tartu, I was a nobody . . . As I was a nobody, I drank, and alternated between moods of depression and periods of high spirits . . . Meanwhile there was one lifebuoy on these stormy seas – I still don't know why, maybe because it was the only time I'd ever glimpsed a prospect of happiness – and that was Berthe . . .

'I was stupid enough to come down to Fécamp last month . . . Berthe gave me some advice . . . Then she added: "Why aren't you more like your brother?"

'Something suddenly occurred to me. I didn't understand why I hadn't thought of it before . . . I could *be* Pietr, whenever I liked!

'A few days later I got a message from him saying he was coming to France and would have need of me.

'I went to Brussels to wait for him. I crossed the tracks and boarded his train from the wrong side. I hid behind the luggage until I saw him get up from his seat to go to the toilet. I got there before he did.

'I killed him! I'd just drunk a litre of Belgian gin. The hardest part was to get his clothes off and then dress him up in mine.'

He was drinking greedily, with an appetite Maigret had never imagined possible.

'At your first meeting in the Majestic, did Mortimer suspect anything?'

'I think he did. But only vaguely. I had only one thing in my mind at that time: to see Berthe again . . . I wanted to tell her the truth . . . I had no real feelings of remorse, yet I felt unable to take advantage of the crime I'd committed . . . There were all sorts of clothes in Pietr's trunk . . . I dressed up as a tramp, the way I'm used to dressing . . . I went out by the back door . . . I sensed that Mortimer was on my tail, and it took me two hours to throw him off the scent . . .

'Then I got a car to drive me to Fécamp . . .

'Berthe was bewildered when I got there . . . And once I was standing in front of her, with her asking me to explain, I didn't have the heart to tell her what I'd done!

'Then you turned up . . . I saw you through the window . . . I told Berthe I was wanted for theft and I asked her to save me. When you'd gone, she said: "Be off with you now! You are bringing dishonour on your brother's house . . ."

'That's right! That's exactly what she said! And I did go off! That's when you and I went back to Paris together . . .

'I went back to Anna . . . We had a row, obviously . . . Screaming and crying . . . Mortimer turned up at midnight, since he'd now seen through the whole thing, and he threatened to kill me unless I took over Pietr's place completely . . .

'It was a huge issue for him . . . Pietr had been his only channel of communication with the gangs . . . Without him, Mortimer would lose his hold over them.

'Back to the Majestic . . . with you right behind me! Someone said something about a dead policeman . . . I could see you'd got a bandage under your jacket . . .

'You'll never know how much life itself disgusted me . . . And the idea that I was condemned to acting the part of my brother for ever more . . .

'Do you remember when you dropped a photograph on the counter of a bar?

'When Mortimer came to the Roi de Sicile, Anna was up in arms . . . She saw it would put paid to her plan . . . She realized my new role would take me away from her . . . Next evening, when I got back to my room at the Majestic, I found a package and a letter . . .'

'A grey off-the-peg suit, and a note from Anna saying she was going to kill Mortimer,' Maigret said. 'And also making an appointment to see you somewhere . . .'

The air was now thick with smoke, which made the room feel warmer. Things looked less clear-cut in the haze. But Maigret spelled it out:

'You came here to kill Berthe . . .'

Hans was having another drink. He finished his glass, gripped the mantelpiece, and said:

'So as to be rid of everybody! Myself included! . . . I'd had enough! . . . All I had in my mind was what my brother would call a Russian idea – to die with Berthe, in each other's arms . . .'

He switched to a different tone of voice.

'That's stupid! You only get that kind of idea from the bottom of a bottle of spirits . . . There was a cop outside the gate . . . I'd sobered up . . . I scouted around . . . That morning I gave a note to the maid, asking my sister-in-law to meet me on the outer pier, saying that if she didn't come in person with some money, I'd be done for . . . That was base of me, wasn't it? But she came . . .'

All of a sudden he put his elbows on the marble mantelpiece and burst into tears, not like a man, but like a child. But, despite his sobs, he went on with his story.

'I wasn't up to it! We were in a dark spot . . . The roar of the sea . . . She was looking worried . . . I told her everything. All of it! Including the murder . . . Yes, changing clothes in the cramped train toilet . . . Then, because she looked like she was going mad with grief, I swore to her that it wasn't true! . . . Wait a moment! I didn't deny the murder! . . . What I retracted was that Pietr was a piece of scum . . . I yelled that I'd made that up to get my own back on him . . . I suppose she believed me . . . *People always believe things like that* . . . She dropped the bag she'd brought with the money in it. Then she said . . . No! She had nothing else to say . . .'

He raised his head and looked at Maigret. His face was contorted, he tried to take a step but couldn't keep his balance and had to steady himself on the mantelpiece.

'Hand me the bottle, pal! . . .'

'Pal' was said with a kind of grumpy affection.

'Hang on! . . . Let me see that photo again . . . The one . . .'

Maigret got out the snapshot of Berthe. That was the only mistake he had made in the whole case: believing that at that moment Hans's mind was on the woman.

'No, not that one. The other one . . .'

The picture of the two boys in their embroidered sailor collar shirts!

The Latvian gazed on it like a man possessed. Inspector

Maigret could only see it upside down, but even so the fairer boy's hero-worship of his brother stood out.

'They took my gun away with my clothes!' Hans blurted out in a blank and steady voice as he looked around the room.

Maigret had gone crimson. He nodded awkwardly towards the bed, where his own service revolver lay.

The native of Pskov let go of the mantelpiece. He wasn't swaying now. He must have summoned up his last scrap of energy.

He went right past the inspector, less than a metre from him. They were both in dressing gowns. They'd drunk rum together.

Their two chairs were still facing each other, on opposite sides of the charcoal heater.

Their eyes met. Maigret couldn't bring himself to look away. He was expecting Hans to stop.

But Hans went on past him as stiff as a pike and sat on the bed, making its springs creak.

There was still a drop left in the second bottle. Maigret took it, clinking its neck against the glass.

He sipped it slowly. Or was he just pretending to drink? He was holding his breath.

Then the bang. He gulped his drink down.

Administratively speaking, the events were as follows:

On . . . 19 November . . . at 10 p.m. verified, an individual by the name of Hans Johannson, born Pskov, Russian Empire, of Estonian nationality, unemployed, residing at Rue du Roi-de-Sicile, Paris, after confessing to the murder of his brother, Pietr Johannson, on . . . November of the same year in the train Étoile du Nord, took his own life by shooting himself in the mouth shortly after his arrest in Fécamp by Detective Chief Inspector Maigret of the Flying Squad.

The 6 mm bullet traversed the palate and lodged in the brain. Death was instantaneous.

As a precaution the body has been taken to the morgue. Receipt of corpse has been acknowledged.

19. *The Injured Man*

The male nurses left, but not before Madame Maigret had treated them to a glass of plum liqueur, which she made herself every year on her summer holiday back home in the country in Alsace.

When she'd closed the door behind them and heard them going down the stairs, she went back into the bedroom with the rose-pattern wallpaper.

Maigret was lying in the double bed under an impressive red silk eiderdown. He looked rather tired; there were little bags under his eyes.

'Did they hurt you?' his wife inquired as she went around, tidying things up in the room.

'Not a lot . . .'

'Can you eat?'

'A bit . . .'

'It's amazing you had the same surgeon as crowned heads and people like Clemenceau and Courteline . . .'

She opened a window to shake out a rug on which a nurse had left the mark of his shoe. Then she went to the kitchen, moved a pot from one ring to another and put the lid at a slant.

'I say, Maigret . . .' she said as she came back into the bedroom.

'What?' he asked.

'Do you really believe that it was a crime of passion?'

'What are you talking about?'

'About the Jewish woman, Anna Gorskin, who's on trial today. A woman from Rue du Roi-de-Sicile who claims she was in love with Mortimer and killed him in a fit of jealousy . . .'

'Ah, that starts today, does it?'

'The story doesn't hold water.'

'Mmm . . . You know, life is a complicated thing . . . You'd better raise my pillow.'

'Might she get an acquittal?'

'Lots of other people have been acquitted.'

'That's what I mean . . . Wasn't she connected to your case?'

'Vaguely . . .' he sighed.

Madame Maigret shrugged.

'A fat lot of use it is being married to an inspector!' she grumbled. With a smile, all the same. 'When there's something going on, I get my news from the door-lady . . . One of her nephews is a journalist, so there!'

Maigret smiled too.

Before having his operation he'd been to see Anna twice, at the Saint-Lazare prison.

The first time she had clawed his face.

The second time she had given him information that led to the immediate arrest at his lodgings in Bagnolet of Pepito Moretto, the murderer of Torrence and José Latourie.

Day after day, and no news! A telephone call now and again, from God knows where, then one fine morning Maigret turns up like a man at the end of his rope, slumps into an armchair and mumbles:

'Get me a doctor . . .'

Now she was happy to be bustling around the flat, pre-tending to be grumpy just for show, stirring the crackling Swiss fries in the pan, hauling buckets of water around, opening and closing windows and asking now and again:

'Time for a pipe?'

Last time she asked she got no answer.

Maigret was asleep. Half of him was buried under the red eiderdown, and his head was sunk deep in a feather pillow, while all these sounds fluttered over his resting face.

In the central criminal court Anna Gorskin was fighting for her life.

In the prison, in a top-security cell, Pepito Moretto knew what fate awaited him. He walked in circles around his cell under the glum gaze of the guard, whose face could only be seen through the grid pattern on the wire screen over the hatch.

In Pskov, an old lady in a folk hat that came down over both cheeks must have been on her way to church in a sled behind a drunken coachman whipping a pony trotting across the snow like a mechanical toy.

OTHER TITLES IN THE SERIES

THE LATE MONSIEUR GALLET
GEORGES SIMENON

Instead of filling out and becoming more comprehensible, was it not more evasive than ever? The face of the man in the tight-fitting jacket was blurred to the point of having nothing human about it.

Instead of the portrait photo, the only tangible and theoretically complete picture of the murder victim that Maigret had, he saw fleeting images which ought to have made up nothing but one and the same man, but refused to be superimposed into a single whole.

The circumstances of Monsieur Gallet's death all seem fake: the name he was travelling under, his presumed profession and, more worryingly, his family's grief. Their haughtiness hides ambiguous feelings about the hapless man. Soon Maigret discovers the real crime buried beneath the lies.

Translated by Anthea Bell

OTHER TITLES IN THE SERIES

THE HANGED MAN OF SAINT-PHOLIEN
GEORGES SIMENON

A first ink drawing showed a hanged man swinging from a gallows on which perched an enormous crow. And there were at least twenty other etchings and pen or pencil sketches that had the same leitmotif of hanging. On the edge of a forest: a man hanging from every branch.

A church steeple: beneath the weathercock, a human body dangling from each arm of the cross.

It all started yesterday. Or did it begin years ago? All Maigret knows is that the shabby traveller he was following has committed suicide in a hotel room. As he delves further, a ten-year-old secret begins to emerge – one that some people will do anything to keep.

Translated by Linda Coverdale

OTHER TITLES IN THE SERIES

THE CARTER OF *LA PROVIDENCE*
GEORGES SIMENON

What was the woman doing here?

In a stable, wearing pearl earrings, her stylish bracelet and white buckskin shoes!

She must have been alive when she got there because the crime had been committed after ten in the evening.

But how? And why? And no one had heard a thing! She had not screamed. The two carters had not woken up.

Maigret is standing in the pouring rain by a canal. A well-dressed woman, Mary Lampson, has been found strangled in a stable nearby. Why did her glamorous, hedonistic life come to such a brutal end here? Surely her taciturn husband, Sir Walter, knows – or maybe the answers lie with the crew of the barge La Providence.

Translated by David Coward

OTHER TITLES IN THE SERIES

THE YELLOW DOG
GEORGES SIMENON

There was an exaggerated humility about her. Her cowed eyes, her way of gliding noiselessly about without bumping into things, of quivering nervously at the slightest word, were the very image of a scullery maid accustomed to hardship. And yet he sensed, beneath that image, glints of pride held firmly in check.

She was anaemic. Her flat chest was not formed to rouse desire. Nevertheless, she was strangely appealing, perhaps because she seemed troubled, despondent, sickly.

In the windswept seaside town of Concarneau, a local wine merchant is shot. In fact, someone is out to kill all the influential men and the entire town is soon sent into a state of panic. For Maigret, the answers lie with the pale, downtrodden waitress Emma, and a strange yellow dog lurking in the shadows...

Translated by Linda Asher